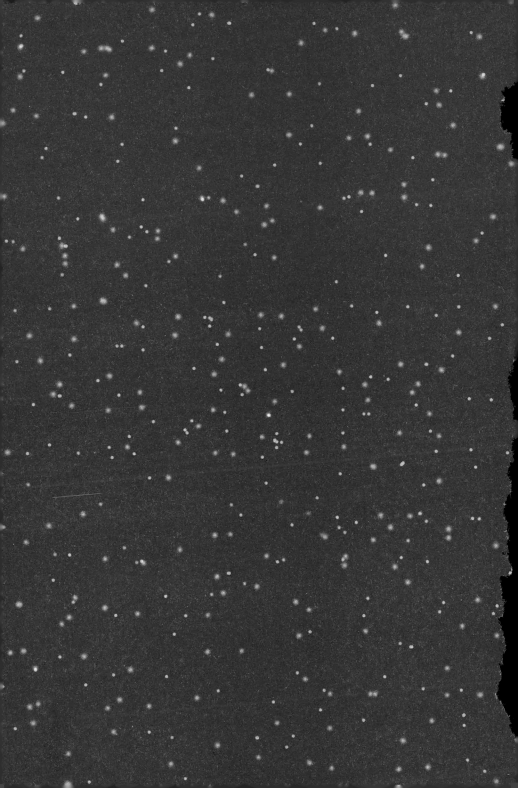

Revenge of
Beneath the
Beyond the
Attack of the
Escape from
Son of

RETURN TO PLANET TAD

TIM CARVELL
Illustrated by Doug Holgate

HARPER
An Imprint of HarperCollinsPublishers

A portion of the text from this book
was originally published in *MAD* magazine.

Return to Planet Tad
Copyright © 2014 E.C. Publications, Inc.
MAD MAGAZINE and all related characters and elements are trademarks
of and © E.C. Publications, Inc.
(s14)

Library of Congress Cataloging-in-Publication Data
Carvell, Tim.
  Return to Planet Tad / Tim Carvell ; illustrated by Doug Holgate. — First
edition.
    pages cm
  Sequel to: Planet Tad.
  Summary: Tad offers commentary on his eighth-grade year via illustrated
blog entries.
  ISBN 978-0-06-226625-5 (hardcover)
  [1. Middle schools—Fiction. 2. Schools—Fiction. 3. Blogs—Fiction.
4. Humorous stories.] I. Holgate, Douglas, illustrator. II. Title.
PZ7.C2537Re 2014   2013043142
[Fic]—dc23   CIP
                                                                      AC

Typography by Erin Fitzsimmons
Illustrations by Doug Holgate
Emoticons by Robert Brook Allen
14 15 16 17 18   CG/RRDH   10 9 8 7 6 5 4 3 2 1
❖
First Edition

For Tom

January

12:01 a.m.

Happy New Year! It's New Year's Day! This morning, the newspaper ran this illustration:

The whole "Baby New Year" thing is weird. I guess the idea is, each year starts out as a tiny baby who somehow ages into an old man. But it's kind of a grim way to welcome the year: "Happy New Year! Think of this year as a newborn baby who will get old and die in a year's time!"

Anyway, welcome to the second year of *Planet Tad*! It's hard to believe it was just one year ago that I started blogging here on my dad's old computer. If you're reading my blog for the first time, I should introduce myself. I'm Tad. I'm thirteen years old, but nearly fourteen. I live in Lakeville with my little sister, Sophie, who's eight, and my mom and dad, who are—

Hang on. Let me go ask my parents how old they are.

12:03 a.m.

My dad is forty-two, and my mom's age is none of your business.

Anyway. I'm very excited to start my second year of blogging. Already, this year is off to a great start: Yesterday, I ran into this girl I like, Jenny Bachman, at the mall, and she asked me if

I wanted to go ice-skating sometime. So I said yes, and we made plans for this Saturday.

The only hitch is, that gives me just three days to learn how to ice-skate. My little sister Sophie has promised to teach me how—just so long as I let her have my dessert all week long. She says it shouldn't take me too long to learn—as she said, "I learned how to skate when I was five, so how hard could it be?"

JANUARY 2 [mood: depressed]

I just got back from my first skating lesson with Sophie, and if I had to sum it up in a word, that word would be:

Ow.

I thought it would be like riding a skateboard,

and it is, except that:

- Instead of the ground, you're moving across slippery ice.
- Instead of a board with wheels, you've got knives strapped to your feet.
- Instead of your driveway, you're in a rink full of people who'll run into you when you fall down, and then shout at you for falling.

After an hour of watching me fall down, Sophie leaned over and said, "It's embarrassing to be seen with you. My rate has gone up to two weeks of desserts." I told her it was a deal.

JANUARY 3 [mood: pain]

Another day of practicing ice-skating with Sophie. The good news is, by the end of the day, I managed to finally start skating and worked up a little speed. The bad news is, Sophie hadn't shown me how to stop or turn yet. So I kind of went into the wall of the rink at full speed. I wound up getting a bloody nose and bleeding all over the ice. And the worst part is, when I went to look for Sophie, she was just skating away, pretending she didn't even know me.

After I went into the bathroom to clean up my face, she was waiting outside. She came over and said, "Are you OK?" And just as I was saying, "Yeah," she finished her sentence: ". . . with going up to three weeks of desserts? Because that's the only way I'm doing this."

JANUARY 4   [mood: hopeful]

Another lesson today. I ache all over, and so far, this has cost me three days of winter vacation and four weeks of desserts—but I can at least hobble around a rink well enough not to make a total fool of myself with Jenny tomorrow.

[mood: crushed]   JANUARY 5

Today I went ice-skating with Jenny. And it started off great: I said, "Hi!" and she gave me a huge smile and said, "Hi! I'm so glad you made it!" But the very next thing she said was, "I hope you don't mind, but I asked my friend Dave to join us." That's when I realized that the big guy standing near her was Dave. He goes to Lakeville East Middle School, and he's, like, a foot taller than me, and has a really deep voice, and according to Jenny, he used to ice-skate competitively. He and Jenny both skate really well, which was good, because they had to help pick me up off the ice a couple of times.

Afterward, Jenny came over and said, "Thanks for coming." And then she whispered, "I was kind of nervous about just hanging out with Dave alone, so it was really good you were here."

JANUARY 6 [mood: tired]

Tonight, my whole family finally took down our Christmas tree. It's strange: as fun as it is putting up the tree, it's sort of depressing taking it down.

We put all the ornaments back into the boxes and very carefully tried to roll up the lights so that they won't be in a big tangle next time, and Sophie and I divided up the candy canes. Candy canes are weird, because the more you suck on one, the sharper and pointier it gets, and the odds of you stabbing yourself in the throat with it just get bigger and bigger. I don't know why you don't see more news stories about kids who died from candy-cane throat stabbings.

Anyway. Once we were done, we put our tree out with the trash. A lot of our neighbors did theirs tonight, too, so if you drive down our street, each house has a dead pine tree in front of it. It's like a scene out of a pine-tree horror movie.

JANUARY 7 [mood: thoughtful]

It's weird that so many cartoon animals—from Mickey Mouse to Woody Woodpecker to Bugs Bunny—all wear white gloves. Are their hands hideous claws? Are they severe germophobes? Or are they constantly committing crimes together, and trying to avoid leaving fingerprints?

Toon Glove Theory #1

In English class today, we learned about haikus. A haiku is a three-line poem that doesn't have to rhyme—the only rule is, it has to have five syllables in the first line, and seven in the second, and then five syllables in the last line. It's the laziest kind of poetry ever.

Anyway, we were all told to write a haiku about something found in nature. I wrote:

Empty soda can
Sits by the side of the road
It contained Pepsi

Our teacher, Mrs. White, said, "This was supposed to be about something found in nature."
And I said, "Pretty much any time I go to a park
or the woods, there's at least one empty soda
can there."

She seemed annoyed, but she couldn't talk more
about it, because Doug Spivak had raised his hand
to ask whether it was OK to hyphenate words in
a haiku. Mrs. White sighed and said, "No, Doug.
If you hyphenate words, then you're just writing
down a sentence."

Which, I just realized, would actually work as a
haiku:

No, Doug. If you hy-
phenate words, then you're just wri-
ting down a sentence.

Anyway. Doug's not very smart. Up until sixth
grade, he thought Alaska and Hawaii were
located in little boxes just below California,

because that's where they are on the maps.

I don't get the saying "you are what you eat." It seems to me like the only people that's true for are cannibals.

So, I came home from school today, and my mom said, "I have two surprises for you!"

Which automatically made me nervous, because my mom never says "I have a surprise for you" when it's something good. And then she said, "Go into the den!" So I went in there, and there was a piano in it. "I was driving home and saw a sign that said 'Piano—Free to Good Home,'" she said. "I don't know why anyone would ever give away a piano, but I couldn't resist!" And I said, "None of us even play the piano." And she smiled and said, "No, not yet." And I said, "Oh, did you sign up for lessons?" And she said, "That's my second surprise for you!"

Yes. My mom has signed me up for piano lessons. I have to go every Sunday starting this weekend.

This is why I hate my mom's surprises.

JANUARY 12 [mood: musical]

My first piano lesson is tomorrow, but I've already figured out how to play three songs, all by myself:

- If you play any two notes on the low end of the piano, it's the theme from *Jaws*.
- If you play any high note over and over and

over again, it's the sound of a serial killer chasing someone through a house.

- If you pound down a bunch of keys all at once, it's someone falling down stairs in a cartoon.

I don't know why people make such a big deal out of composing music. It turns out, it's pretty easy.

JANUARY 13 [mood: tired]

So, today was my first piano lesson. My dad drove me. I asked him if I really had to go, and he said, "Give it a shot! Sophie hated oboe lessons at first, but she loves them now!" And I said, "You realize that I'm nothing like Sophie, right?" And he said, "Yeah, I do. But you still have to go."

My lesson was with a guy named Mr. Fitzhoff. I showed him the three songs I'd figured out, and he kind of frowned, and then he said, "You know, I can always tell when someone has real, innate musical talent." And I said, "Do I?" And he said, "No."

He showed me which keys are which, and

taught me how to play "Mary Had a Little Lamb."
When I got home, I showed Sophie. She said, "Oh,
yeah! I remember learning to play that on the
oboe! When I was *six*."

JANUARY 16 [mood: disappointed]

Our town has something called an "Elks Lodge"
in it. I remember being really disappointed when I
was a kid to find out that it's just a room where old
men hang out, and not a hotel for elks.

JANUARY 20 [mood: grumpy]

Today was another piano lesson. It went fine. Mr. Fitzhoff said that I should really practice more. I asked him how I'd know if I was practicing enough, and he said, "Well, when you can play more than three notes in a row correctly, that'd be a start." So that's good to know.

[mood: starstruck] JANUARY 21

In class today, I learned that the Big Dipper is part of a constellation called "Ursa Major," which means "big bear," because apparently the Greeks thought the stars made the shape of a bear. Which means they looked at this:

And saw this:
I dunno. Either
the Greeks were
really creative, or
bears used to look
really different.

Had a bad time in art class today. There's nothing awk-warder in the world than trying to use lefty scissors when you're right-handed.

Piano lesson again today. I don't think Mr. Fitzhoff

likes me. Mainly because when I showed up, he sighed and said, "Oh, right. You." He said that I really should practice a lot more if I want to get any better at playing the piano. He told me that, when he was a kid, he practiced for two hours every day. And I said, "Wow. So you must've really wanted to be a piano teacher when you grew up, huh?" And he paused for a really long time, and then said, "Sure."

JANUARY 28 [mood: crafty]

Tonight at dinner, my mom said, "Tad, I don't notice you practicing the piano very much." And I said, "Yeah, I keep meaning to, but I never have the time." And she said, "You watched all of *The Lord of the Rings* on TV last night. You could've practiced then." And I was just about to say, "Nobody wants to hear me practice," when I had an idea.

Tonight, after dinner, I sat down and practiced the piano. I practiced "Mary Had a Little Lamb" over and over for a solid two hours. I never played it right once.

JANUARY 29 [mood: devious]

Another night of practicing. If anything, I'm making sure that "Mary Had a Little Lamb" is sounding even worse. My mom came in and asked me if Mr. Fitzhoff had taught me any other songs. I told her no, and then went back to playing it wrong.

[mood: determined] JANUARY 30

Still more practicing. Tonight, my mom was in the next room, watching TV, and I could tell my playing was beginning to annoy her, because she started turning the TV volume up. So I practiced even louder. And the more she turned up the TV, the louder I practiced.

JANUARY 31 [mood: triumphant]

Today, I sat down and practiced again—I've gotten to the point where I can play "Mary Had a Little

Lamb" so badly, it doesn't even sound like a song anymore. After about half an hour, my mom came in and said, "Tad? Honey? How much more do you think you'll be practicing today?" And I said, "My teacher says it sometimes takes years just to master one song." And her eye twitched a little, and then she said, "You know what? I'm thinking maybe music isn't where your gifts lie. Maybe we should find another hobby for you." So I acted all sad, and then I went up to my room and made a sign:

I think we might be using it soon.

February

So in two weeks, my school's going to have its big eighth-grade semiformal dance. They have it every February in our school gym, and there's always some lame theme—last year, it was "One Moment in Time." The year before, it was "Hawaiian Luau," which ended really badly when a tiki torch got a little too close to a fake grass hut; you can still see

the fire damage over by the bleachers. Anyway, we had an assembly today where the student council announced that, for the first time, they were going to let students suggest themes for the dance. They put up a suggestion box, and I've already come up with a few possibilities:

- "Dancing Without the Stars"
- "*Alien vs. Predator*"
- "Come Dressed as Your Favorite Ewok"
- "Let's All Pretend This Isn't the Room Where We Played Kickball Three Hours Ago"

FEBRUARY 2 [mood: cold]

This morning was Groundhog Day. On the news, they said that there was a huge blizzard in Pennsylvania, so they had to get a massive snowplow and clear the ground, just in order to get the groundhog out of his hole.

I feel like, if you have to clear five feet of snow in order to find the groundhog, you already know the answer to whether winter is over or not.

This afternoon, I told my mom that she needed to take me to the store to get the new *Zombie Artillery* game, and she said, "You know, Tad, you could say *please* when you ask me to do a favor. It's always good to be polite. You catch more flies with honey than with vinegar." I pointed out that actually, you'd probably catch more flies with dog poop than you would with either honey or vinegar. And she said, "OK, you've sort of missed the point."

So today, my mom came into the living room and found Chuck and me playing *Zombie Artillery*, and she said, "What is that?" And I said, "It's the game we got the other day." And Chuck said, "Here, look: I'm throwing a grenade into that zombie's head before he can eat that lady's spine, so I can get double points." But before he could finish, my mom turned off the game and said, "I don't want you playing this. It's too violent." I'm not sure how my mom bought me a video game called *Zombie Artillery* and didn't realize that it involved shooting zombies with guns, but moms can be sort of weird sometimes.

. Anyway, she went to the store to return the game, saying, "I'm sorry, you're just too young for this." So Chuck and I hung out and watched some police show about a guy who killed his victims by beating them up with their own severed limbs and then dissolved them in tubs of acid.

FEBRUARY 5 [mood: disappointed]

At lunch today the student-council president, Stacy Ramos, came over to our cafeteria table and told us what the theme for the semiformal's going to be: "Enchantment Under the Sea." And I said,

"So, the idea is that we're all underwater?" And she said, "Uh-huh!" And I said, "So we're, like, the victims of a tragic shipwreck, trapped on the bottom of the ocean?" And she said, "No. We're all alive." And I said, "Not for long if we're underwater. Maybe you should go with a more accurate theme, like, 'Asphyxiation Under the Sea.'" And she got all annoyed and walked away.

I still think "Asphyxiation Under the Sea" would be an awesome theme.

FEBRUARY 6 [mood: hopeful]

Today Chuck came up with a good idea: He and I sit near these two girls, Sara Collins and Heather Blankenship, in art class, and we sort of joke around with them when Ms. Booker isn't looking. And Chuck suggested that maybe we could each ask one of them to go to the dance, and then we could all go together as a double date. So tomorrow after class, we're going to ask them. I'm a little nervous, but as Chuck said, "The worst they can say is no, right?"

So we asked Sara and Heather today. Chuck asked Sara, and I asked Heather. Afterward, Chuck said, "Well, she said she was flattered, but that she really just kind of thinks of me as a friend."

And I told him how my conversation went: I said, "Do you want to go to the dance next Friday?" And Heather said, "Yes!" And then she said, "Oh! You mean with you? Oh. Ew! No. Sorry. I didn't mean to say *ew*. It's just that the idea of going to the dance with you makes me say that. Because I really, really, really, really would not want to do that. Ew."

And Chuck said, "Man, that's so much worse than just *no*."

I don't understand the expression "a square peg in

a round hole." A square peg would fit just fine in a round hole, as long as the hole was large enough.

I feel bad for Chuck. I gave up on asking girls to the dance, but he's still trying. So far, he's asked eight different girls to go to the semiformal with him, and they've all said no. (Well, actually, he only asked six girls. The Markowitz twins came up to him in the hallway and said, "We hear you're asking girls to the dance, and we thought you should know, if you're thinking of asking either of us, the answer is no." Afterward, I said to him, "That was pretty arrogant of them, to just think that you were going

to ask them," and he said, "Yeah. But they *were* the next ones on my list.")

In study hall, Chuck overheard some girls talking about how they were planning on going as a group, and he suggested to me and Kevin that maybe we should just go as a group, too. And I was about to say no, but then I remembered: this Friday, my mom's book club is coming over to the house. And if I had to choose between a night at a dance with Chuck and Kevin, and a night at home surrounded by all my mom's friends, not being allowed to watch TV in the living room, and hearing my mom's friend Bev's weird, crazy laugh over and over again, I'd choose the dance, anytime. So I guess we're all going under the sea on Friday.

FEBRUARY 12 [mood: confused]

Sophie is getting ready for Valentine's Day at her school. She bought cards that have that stupid poem, "Roses are red, violets are blue, sugar is sweet, and so are you." I hate that poem, because it's not even true—violets are violet. Basically, the poem amounts to, "Hi, I'm either an idiot or a liar, and I love you."

My dad got my mom a box of chocolates as an early Valentine's Day present. She said I could have one, but the one I picked tasted like it was filled with cherry cough syrup. It was disgusting. I think if I ever ran a chocolate company, I wouldn't make my chocolates all fancy looking. They'd just be little cubes with writing on top that said exactly what was inside them.

The dance is tomorrow night, and I've realized I'm not exactly sure what *semiformal* means. At first I thought it meant you could show up just wearing the top half of a tuxedo:

But I asked Stacy Ramos, and she tells me it means you have to wear a coat and tie. "It's a dress code," she said. "They won't let you in without a tie on. No exceptions." And I said, "What if you're a girl?" And she said, "No, only if you're a boy. No exceptions for boys." And I said, "What if there's a fire—would they let the firefighters in without ties on?" And she said, "Yes. No exceptions for boys, except firefighters." And I said, "What if you have a really big neck goiter, and you can't find a tie that fits around it?" And she said, "I'm leaving now."

6:46 p.m.

Well, tonight's the big dance. I came home and got my best khakis and sports coat on, and because I can't tie a tie, my dad stood behind me and tied it for me. My mom kept saying, "You look so handsome! Doesn't he look handsome, Sophie?" And Sophie said, "No. He looks like Tad." I'm heading out now! Wish me luck!

9:15 p.m.

Aaaaaaaaaaaaaaaaaaaaaaaaaaaaaaaaaaaargh.

I got to the dance tonight, and at first, everything was OK. I mean, it wasn't great, because I'd kind of forgotten a dance involves actually dancing, which is something I can't really do. So I was just hanging out near the snack table with Chuck when Varya Kumar, who's the vice president of the student council—but actually kind of cool and smart and nice—came over and said, "Why aren't you dancing?" And I said, "I'm not really good at it." And she said, "C'mon! I helped to organize this dance. It'll look really bad if no one's dancing. Tell you what: I'll teach you how."

So we went out into the middle of the dance floor, and she started to teach me. "Just move your feet to the beat," she said. And so I started, and she said, "No, you're moving your feet to every word of the song. Just listen for the beat." And I said, "Which part's the beat?" And she sighed and said,

"Just watch me and do what I do." And so I started to do that, and she sort of laughed, and then she apologized and said, "No! It's just . . . you're doing really well. But maybe you'd do better with a slow song. Tell you what: I'll find you when a slow song comes on, and we can practice dancing some more then." And that's when I realized: Varya wasn't just teaching me to dance—she'd been flirting with me the whole time.

I went back and told Chuck, and he said, "That's awesome! You should go fix your tie real quick—it's a little crooked." So I left the gym and went to the bathroom to fix my tie. But before I did that, I realized my hair was sticking up in back, so I turned on the faucet to put a little water on it, and the faucet wound up spraying my pants so it looked like I wet myself. I tried to dry my pants off with the hand dryer, but I couldn't bring it down to pants level. So then I tried using toilet paper, which didn't really dry my pants much at all, but did leave tiny bits of paper all over my pants. So I untucked my shirt to hide the wet spot, but then I realized that one of my shirt tails had an ink spot on it from when I left a pen uncapped in my pocket the last time I wore it. So

I hid that by rebuttoning my shirt, but off by one button, to make that shirttail shorter so it'd fit under my sports coat. And then I remembered: I still hadn't fixed my crooked tie. So I started to try to adjust it, and the more I messed with it the worse it looked, until the little end of the tie was completely in front of the big part, and I started sliding the knot down the tie and back up again, and wound up accidentally untying it. And because I couldn't get back into the dance without a tie on, I had to retie it with the only knot I know, which is the one you use to tie your shoes, but it didn't really look right at all:

Before

After

I walked back into the gym and found Chuck, and I started to say, "Hey, is it noticeable that—" when Chuck said, "Whoa! What happened to your tie? And your shirt? And did you wet your pants?" But before I could tell him anything, a slow song came on, and I saw Varya looking around the dance floor for me, and I realized I had two choices: let her see me looking like a mess, or run. And so I ran. And I kept going until I could call my parents and have them pick me up, and now I'm home.

FEBRUARY 16 [mood: relieved]

9:15 a.m.
Awesome! I just woke up and found that Varya had sent me an instant message:

> **Hi, Tad. Chuck explained where you went, and I totally understand. Sorry you had to leave, and I hope you're doing OK.**

I'm not sure what that means, exactly, but I'm glad that Chuck was smart enough to cover for me. Hang on. I'm gonna write back and ask what, exactly, Chuck told her.

9:17 a.m.
Ugh. Here's Varya's response:

He said you got diarrhea.

I'm really going to have to talk to Chuck about what constitutes a "good alibi."

FEBRUARY 17 [mood: cheated]

Well, there's a major blizzard going on outside, which ordinarily would be great news, because it'd mean that tomorrow would be a snow day at school. But it turns out, tomorrow's Presidents' Day, so we already have the day off. So it's just a waste of a perfectly good blizzard.

Anyway, our whole family is stuck indoors, and my mom is insisting on us having family fun time. We all played Scrabble for a little while, but it's no fun to play with Sophie. (In our first game, my dad started by playing *CAT* for ten points, and then Sophie played *AQUEDUCT* for 116 points.) Then we switched to Sorry! because, as my dad muttered to me, "If your sister's going to beat us all, I want it to be a game where she apologizes first."

So just now at dinner, my mom said, "Tad, I hope you enjoyed your three-day weekend. Did you get all your homework done?"

And I suddenly remembered: because of Presidents' Day, everyone in our social studies class was assigned to pick one president, and give a presentation tomorrow on all the achievements of his administration. I'd totally forgotten about it, and was beginning to panic, when Sophie looked up and said, "You can pick any president you want?" And I said, "Yeah." And she said, "And you just have to talk about what they did as president?" And I said, "That's right." And she said, "Do William Henry Harrison." I asked her why, and she said, "You'll see."

So I'm about to start researching him. Hopefully, I won't be up all night working.

Today in social studies class, I watched as everyone in my class gave massive presentations about their presidents, taking a really long time to list all the bills they signed and the treaties they negotiated and the wars they fought. And then it was my turn, and I stood up and said, "William Henry Harrison caught pneumonia at his inauguration, and died one month later. The end."

Sometimes, it's good to have a little sister who's a genius.

Today was a good day—our school had its eighth grade spelling bee, and I won!

The whole spelling bee took nearly two hours. Some kids got knocked out of the running immediately—Doug Spivak, who's the dumbest kid in my class, was knocked out because he spelled *house* with a *d*. And Jeff Garber fought with the teacher for ten minutes when he misspelled *fanciest* as *fanceist*. He kept saying, "But everyone always says the rule is '*i* before *e*, except after *c*'!" He sort of had a point, actually.

In the end, it came down to me and Emily Davis. It was sort of intense. For twenty solid minutes, we kept going back and forth and back and forth, spelling words, until she finally misspelled *pterodactyl*. In order to win, I had to spell *fluorescent*, and for a second, I considered spelling it wrong, because it seemed sort of weird to beat a girl in a contest. But then I remembered that Emily is actually really snotty and mean, and I went ahead and spelled the word.

Afterward, I went up to her and said, "Hey, you did really well. Either of us could've won." And she said, "Your fly was open the whole time," and walked away. That made me feel a whole lot less bad about beating her.

So today, my English teacher, Mrs. White, presented me with my prize for winning the spelling bee: a dictionary. Which is sort of an odd prize for being the best speller. You'd think they would give the dictionary to the class's worst speller.

She also let me in on the downside of winning the school's spelling bee: now I have to compete in the regional spelling bee. Which means I'm going to have to get up early next Thursday and be driven over to the civic center to compete against other schools' spelling-bee winners. She gave me a folder with a list of words to study, but I figure that I'll be OK—I'm a pretty good speller.

FEBRUARY 22 [mood: worried]

Uh-oh. Today, our school's principal, Dr. Evans, came up to me in the lunchroom and said, "Here's our big speller! Are you *r-e-a-d-y* for the competition?" And then she laughed at her own joke, and then she said, very seriously: "You're preparing for the spelling bee, though, right? You're studying the words? Because ours is the only middle school in the region that's never won one." And I said, "Yep." And she said, "OK, good. Because all the other principals have at least one spelling-bee trophy. All of them. All of them but me." And she seemed to be about to cry, so I told her I was studying as hard as I could. And she said, "Excellent! I'm counting on you! I mean, the school's counting on you!"

Anyway, when I got home, I opened up the folder and looked over the list of spelling-bee words. The list had words on it like *ganglionitis, xoanon, miscible,* and *dolorimeter.* I had to look up

what all of them mean. *Dolorimeter,* it turns out, is an instrument that measures pain and suffering. I think that right now, I would score very high on a dolorimeter.

FEBRUARY 24 [mood: disconsolate]

Ugh. I've just spent the last three hours making flash cards for all the spelling-bee words. I'm trying to remember the words by putting them into sentences, but it's not easy. A lot of my sentences are things like, "Tad really hoped that *polydactyly* wouldn't be part of the spelling bee."

[mood: sleepy] FEBRUARY 26

Today after English class, Mrs. White pulled me aside and said, "Dr. Evans asked me to check with you and make sure you're studying all the spelling bee words." I told her that I was, and she looked really relieved. She said, "She's been talking about the spelling bee a lot, you know. A lot."

FEBRUARY 27 [mood: anxious]

Tonight's the last night before the spelling bee. So

I spent another night studying the words, until I fell asleep on top of a pile of flash cards. Then I dreamed that I was at the spelling bee, and all my competitors were gigantic bees who could spell. It was terrifying.

FEBRUARY 28 [mood: miserable]

The spelling bee went calamitously. Ruinously. Grievously.

All of which, by the way, are words I can spell. What I couldn't spell, it turned out, was the very first word I was asked. Which was *janitor*. I guess I was just really nervous, but as soon as I got the word, I stood up there behind the microphone, staring out at my parents, and my sister, and Dr. Evans in the audience, and very confidently said: *"G."*

And then I tried to pretend that I'd said it like, "Gee . . ." and said, *"J,"* but the judges hit the bell that meant I was out, and I had to leave the stage. I was the very first contestant to lose.

My parents were really nice about it. They hugged me and said they were all proud of me, anyway. And Dr. Evans said, "Yes, Tad. We're all very proud of you." But it was hard not to notice that she was saying it through clenched teeth, and that she had the spelling-bee program crumpled into a tiny ball, clutched in her fist.

As we left for the parking lot, one of the principals of another school came up to Dr. Evans and said, "Well, you gave it your best shot, Ganet." Which was weird, because Dr. Evans's first name is Janet.

Oh. I just got that.

Man, principals can be *mean.*

March

We went out for Chinese food tonight, and we all got fortune cookies. My fortune had this on the back of it:

LUCKY NUMBERS ARE
3 18 34 35 46 61

And my first thought was, I should play the lottery with these numbers! And then I looked at my mom's cookie, and realized that she also got a list of lucky numbers, and it was completely different. And so did my dad, and my sister. And if we all played the lottery, at least three of us would lose.

I'm beginning to suspect that fortune cookies are just a really elaborate scheme by the people who run the lottery.

MARCH 2 [mood: annoyed]

Tonight I went to the grocery store with my mom, which is always a huge mistake. My mom loves shopping with coupons, so any trip to the store is about running up and down the aisles trying to find the exact size of something she has a coupon for. Coupons kind of make my mom crazy. Like, tonight, we bought a thirty-six-ounce bottle of ranch dressing, even though no one in our family likes ranch dressing, but my mom said, "With this coupon, it's practically free!"

Three months from now, we will throw out that bottle of ranch dressing. I just know it.

My mom's watching one of those TV cooking-competition shows where the chefs have to make a meal out of a bunch of random ingredients they've been given.

I think if I were ever on one of those shows, and I knew I was going to lose, I'd put all the food in a blender with some anchovies and some chocolate chips, just to watch the judges try and eat it.

St. Patrick's Day is coming up, so McDonald's is selling Shamrock Shakes. I bet a real shamrock shake would taste disgusting.

Today was my birthday! I'm officially fourteen years old! That's two dog years! I pointed out to my mom that I'm just one year away from being able to get my learner's permit, and she said, "Don't remind me."

But the best part is, I've been asking my parents for a cell phone for a while now, and for my birthday, they got me one. (Well, actually, they didn't really get me one. My dad got my mom a new one, and she gave me her old one. Believe me: if I were allowed to pick out my cell phone, it would be newer, and be able to play games, and it wouldn't be purple or glittery.)

MARCH 9　　　[mood: connected]

At lunch today, I showed my new phone to Kevin and Chuck. They mostly just made fun of it for being all sparkly and purple. Chuck looked at it and said, "So who are you going to call on it? Grimace? Barney the dinosaur?" And then Kevin said,

"Yeah! Or maybe you could call . . ." And then he got stuck, because there really aren't that many purple characters.

HELLO? YES, THIS IS HE!

MARCH 10   [mood: embarrassed]

I got my first phone call on my cell phone today. I was at Chuck's house for his birthday party, and my mom called to let me know that she'd be a little late picking me up. It was nice of her to call, but let's just say that a room filled with your friends is not the best place to find out that the ringtone your mom put on her phone was the cast of *Glee* singing "Don't Stop Believing."

So I downloaded some new ringtones. My favorite is one that sounds like Chewbacca. Now I just really want someone to call me so I can show it off.

So today at school, Chuck pointed something out to me: my parents said I could call only them on my phone. But they never said anything about texting. So we started using our phones to text back and forth during class. It was a lot of fun, although we did almost get caught during health class. Mrs. Kankel was demonstrating how to perform CPR on a rubber doll, and Chuck texted me:

> if staying alive = letting mrs k do that 2 me,
> pls let me die

I started laughing so hard that I had to pretend I was coughing, and Mrs. Kankel had to come over and keep asking me, over and over again, if I wanted her to give me the Heimlich maneuver. (I kind of suspect that, after all these years of teaching the Heimlich maneuver, Mrs. Kankel is desperate to get a chance, just once, to use it on somebody.)

MARCH 14 [mood: tired]

Can't type much today. Spent the whole day at school texting my way through class, and now my thumbs are sore.

MARCH 15

Today I found out that I can update my blog from my phone! I can post here using text messages, so long as I don't use more than 140 charac

MARCH 18 [mood: nauseated]

Today at school, the cafeteria was selling green hamburgers. Our principal, Dr. Evans, said, "Oh, is this because yesterday was St. Patrick's Day?" And

BIOHAZARD

one of the cafeteria ladies said, "Yesterday was St. Patrick's Day?" And then Dr. Evans shut the cafeteria line down.

MARCH 19 [mood: psyched]

I'm really getting the most out of my new cell phone. I've signed up for text-messaging services that'll send me my horoscope, the weather, and a fun celebrity fact every day. So I know that it's going to rain, that my Saturn is in Capricorn, and that someone named Casper Van Dien plays the trumpet. I need to figure out ways to work those into conversations.

[mood: happy] MARCH 20

Oh, man, I signed up for this joke-a-day text-message service, and just got a great one: "Why don't nuns floss?"

Whoops, hang on—my parents are calling me downstairs. Something about the phone bill. Be right back.

Um, in case you've been wondering where I've been for the last week: I kind of had my computer privileges taken away. Along with pretty much every other privilege. But I learned some valuable things during that time.

Like that my parents didn't get a text-message plan for my phone.

And that text messages apparently cost twenty cents apiece.

And that, if you multiply twenty cents by 637, you get $127.40.

Anyway. I got my phone back, on two conditions. The first is that the only thing I can do with it is talk to my parents. And the second is that my ringtone has to be "I'm a Little Teapot." My parents are kind of evil geniuses sometimes.

At the mall today, in the atrium where they usually have "Santa's Workshop" every December, they had an "Easter Wonderland," where a guy in an Easter Bunny suit sat on a chair and kids could sit on his lap. I don't get what the purpose of that is. Like, when I was a kid, and you went to visit Santa, there was a reason for it: so you could tell him what you wanted for Christmas. That was the whole point—otherwise, you'd just be hanging out with some fat, beardy stranger. But there's no real reason for you to go talk to the Easter Bunny. You know, and he knows, that he's going to bring you Easter candy. So what's there for a kid to discuss with a seven-foot-tall rabbit? The weather?

If *Two and a Half Men* were really about two guys and their half a friend, I would totally watch it.

[mood: busted]   **MARCH 30**

Well, tonight was the end of an era in our family. For the past few years, Sophie has pretended to believe in the Easter Bunny, because she figured that my parents would bring her more candy if they thought she actually believed in him. But tonight, when my dad came home from the grocery store, my sister and I were helping to unpack the bags, and Sophie took out some sacks of Easter candy. And before she could put them back, my mom saw her and said, "Well, Sophie, I guess it's time you knew: there is no Easter Bunny. We're the ones who bring you the candy." And Sophie sighed and said, "Yeah. I know. I've known for a while now." And my mom said, "Oh, good. We were actually getting kind of worried about having an eight-year-old who believed in the Easter Bunny."

MARCH 31 [mood: guilty]

Ate some Easter candy today. My least favorite Easter candy has to be the Peep. Every year, I eat half of one, and then I remember that eating a Peep is sort of like eating an enormous sugary booger rolled in sand. I pointed that out to Sophie this morning, and asked if she wanted to trade any of her candy for my Peeps, and she said, "Well, no, not now that you said that booger thing."

April

Today in math, Doug Spivak raised his hand and said, "May I be excused? I wet my pants." And sure enough, his pants were soaking wet. And Mrs. Kaplan said, "Goodness, Douglas! Of course!" And then Doug said, "April Fools! It's just water!" And Mrs. Kaplan said, "Yes. But your pants are still soaking wet." And Doug stood there for a second, then said, "Oh . . . yeah." And Mrs. Kaplan just sighed and said, "Go dry yourself off."

After English class today, Mrs. White asked me to stay behind. She's in charge of the school play, and she said she thought I'd be perfect for it. I told her I wasn't really interested. And then she told me that only two boys have signed up for the play this year, and she needs at least four more. And then she pointed out that my grades this quarter have been pretty lousy, because I kind of skipped reading *The Scarlet Letter* and then tried to make up for it by watching the movie, but I accidentally rented *The Scarlet Pimpernel* instead, and there's a big difference between the two.

And then she said how much she'd hate to see me have to do summer school, and that my being in the play *might* make her feel like "accidentally" increasing my grade a little.

So I said yes.

I think I got blackmailed today by a teacher. I didn't even know they were allowed to do that.

APRIL 3   [mood: hopeful]

So today, I had my audition for the play. It's called *Our Town*, and we all did a scene as the main character, George. The play's about how George falls in love with a girl named Emily, and she dies. Spoiler alert. Sorry.

In order to get a small part, I tried to be as bad an actor as I could. But what I forgot was, three of the other guys also didn't want to be there, so they did even worse. Ben Irvin pretended he didn't understand how scripts work, so he kept reading

his character name at the beginning of his lines, saying things like "George hello" and "George thank you." Mike Fine pretended he had a stutter for his whole audition. And Noah Simons whispered all his lines, which drove Miss Engel nuts.

The cast list goes up tomorrow. I really want to just be, like, "Townsperson Number Two," but really, so long as I'm not George, I'll be happy.

APRIL 4   [mood: disappointed]

Well, the list is up, and I'm George.

Argh.

Meanwhile, one of the guys who actually *wanted* to be in the play was so angry that I got the part that he quit. Miss Engel said that was OK—she'll just recast his part with a girl, so the townsperson named Sam is now called Samantha.

[mood: scared]   **APRIL 5**

Today, Jay Shepard, who's this huge, hulking kid in our grade, bumped into me in the hallway, twice. I couldn't figure it out until I remembered that Jay's girlfriend, Abigail Wallace, is playing Emily. Who I kiss during the play.

So I guess Jay is jealous. The funny part is, I don't even like Abigail. She always smells like onions, and she's got a lazy eye, so when you talk to her, it's like she's looking at someone who's behind and a little to the left of you. It's creepy.

Although I guess I can't tell Jay that.

APRIL 8   [mood: scared-er]

Today we had the first read-through of the play. It was OK, I guess, except that Jay Shepard sat in the

audience staring at me the whole time, which kind of made it hard to concentrate on the play. I was really nervous when it

came to the part where Abigail and I are supposed to kiss, but I guess Abigail didn't want to kiss me, either, because instead of doing it, she just said, "Mwah!"

I was worried that Miss Engel would stop and make us actually do it, but she said it was fine if Abigail didn't want to kiss me every time in rehearsal, and Abigail blurted out, "Oh, good!"

I was relieved, too, but I kind of wish she hadn't said it quite so quickly.

Meanwhile, Mike Fine's no longer in the play, because he fell off his bike and broke his collarbone. Miss Engel gave his part to another one of the girls, so the character of Joe is now Josephine.

APRIL 9 [mood: tired]

Rehearsals are going OK, I think. I've learned almost all of my lines, and I've almost managed to forget that Jay Shepard is staring at me the whole time I'm rehearsing. Also, I figured out that if you just concentrate on Abigail's right eye, it's almost as if she's looking right at you.

The bad news is, Noah Simons and Fred Carter are both out of the play—Noah's family moved, and Fred got suspended for cheating. But Miss Engel says it's OK. She promoted two more girls, and the characters of Simon and Howie are now Simone and Holly.

In science class today, Mr. Webster told us that no two snowflakes are exactly alike. Which, unless someone has been out there, quietly checking every single snowflake, just seems like a lie.

Sometimes I feel bad for Doug Spivak. Today in science, we had a pop quiz: we were given drawings of all the kinds of dinosaurs we'd studied, and asked to give the name for each one. Doug raised his hand and said, "Um, should these be boys' names? Or girls' names? Or should they just be names that would work either way, like Alex or Casey?" And Mr. Webster stood there for what felt like a solid minute, trying not to laugh, and then he said, "You're supposed to write their *scientific* names." And Doug said, "Oh. So, like, Professor Alex, and Doctor Casey?" And Mr. Webster told him he could just hand his quiz in and go sit quietly in the library.

APRIL 16 [mood: nervous]

OK, *Our Town* is three days away from opening, and the play's getting a little weird now. Ben Irvin, who played George's father, can't be in it because he has to go to his grandma's funeral. And Eddie Lee, who played Emily's father, fell off the stage and broke his leg. So Miss Engel decided that both George's and Emily's fathers are now dead, and assigned all their fathers' lines to their mothers. The girls who played their mothers tried to complain, but Miss Engel looked really frantic, so they kept their mouths shut.

I'm the last boy left in the play. Miss Engel told me to be very, very careful for the next few days. I didn't tell her that there's probably a fifty-fifty chance Jay Shepard may take me out of commission before opening night.

APRIL 17　　　[mood:　　　sleepless]

I can't sleep. Our dress rehearsal's tomorrow, and Miss Engel says that Abigail and I have to kiss during it.

I don't know what I expected the first time I kissed a girl to be like, but I'm pretty sure it didn't involve doing it onstage, in front of an audience, including her angry boyfriend, while ignoring her lazy eye, in order to get a passing grade in English.

APRIL 18 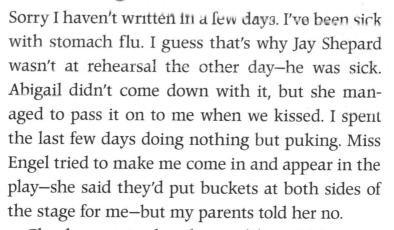 [mood: relieved]

Woo-hoo! It's a miracle! Jay Shepard wasn't at rehearsal today! I don't know where he was, but I kissed Abigail, and it all went fine! (Except that she smelled like onions, which was kind of gross.)

After rehearsal, I asked Abigail where Jay was, and she said she didn't know—he left early today. I don't care why—all I know is, today was a very, very, very lucky day for me.

[mood: puking] APRIL 22

Sorry I haven't written in a few days. I've been sick with stomach flu. I guess that's why Jay Shepard wasn't at rehearsal the other day—he was sick. Abigail didn't come down with it, but she managed to pass it on to me when we kissed. I spent the last few days doing nothing but puking. Miss Engel tried to make me come in and appear in the play—she said they'd put buckets at both sides of the stage for me—but my parents told her no.

Chuck went to the play, and he said it was a

little weird. Miss Engel came out at the beginning and announced, "This play is set in a town where all the men have been abducted by aliens," and

Abigail read all my lines, preceded by, "If George were here, I bet he'd say this right now."

Chuck said it made the whole thing a little more interesting, actually.

APRIL 24   [mood: nervous]

8:26 p.m.

So I'm a little nervous about tomorrow. It's Take Your Sons and Daughters to Work Day, and usually my mom takes me to the retirement home where she works as a nurse, and I spend the day hanging out with old people and eating cookies and watching TV.

But this year's the first year that Sophie's old enough to participate, so my mom's going to take her to her job, and my dad is going to take me to his job, which is . . .

Ugh. I can't remember what my dad's job is called. He keeps telling me, and I keep forgetting. Hang on. I'll go ask him.

8:31 p.m.

Systems-integration consulting analyst. He's a systems-integration consulting analyst. I'm not sure what that means, but it's what he is. Maybe, by the end of the day tomorrow, I'll actually know what that means.

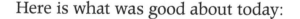

APRIL 25   [mood: traumatized]

Here is what was good about today:

1.   My dad's office has a cool-looking fountain in the lobby.

2. My dad's office also has a machine
that makes hot chocolate, for free.

   That is all that was good about today. Here is
what was bad about today:

1. I still don't know what my dad's job
is. I spent the whole day at his office,
and as best I can tell, "systems-
integration consulting analyst"
means "you sit in a lot of meetings
and talk about boring stuff I don't
understand."
2. I had to sit in a lot of meetings about
boring stuff I didn't understand. I
felt sort of bad for my dad, actually.
I kept falling asleep during the
meetings, because I didn't understand
what anyone was talking about. He
tried to explain some of the stuff to
me at lunch, but then I wound up
falling asleep during the explanations.
I told him, "I'm sorry. It's just that
your job's really boring." And he said,
"Yeah. I know."

3. After lunch, my dad decided that he couldn't make me sit through any more meetings, so he said I could hang out in an empty conference room and play with my GamePort XL. Which sounded perfect, but it turns out, I wasn't the only kid there for Take Your Sons and Daughters to Work Day. My dad's boss had brought his seven-year-old son Trevor in, and he was also in the conference room. And as soon as my dad walked away, Trevor leaned over and whispered, "Let me play with your GamePort." And I said, "No. I'm playing on it." And he said, "Your dad works for my dad. That means you have to do what I say." And I said, "I'm pretty sure that's not how things work." And he said, "If you don't let me have it, I'll tell my dad that you taught me swearwords." And I said, "What swearwords do you even know?"

It turns out, he knows all of them, plus some others I'd never heard before. So I had to let him play with the GamePort all afternoon, plus go and get him cups of hot chocolate.

4. Also, when Trevor spilled a full cup of hot chocolate on the carpet, he made me take the blame for it. His dad came in and said, "Who did this?" and I was about to say, "Trevor," when Trevor started mouthing swearwords at me, and I said, "It's my fault. Sorry."

In the car ride home, I told my dad about Trevor, and he said, "Yep. Sounds like he takes after his dad." I told my dad that I never want to go to Take Your Sons and Daughters to Work Day again. I said, "I thought I'd find out what it was like to be an adult and have a job. And instead, I was somewhere I didn't want to be, bored out of my head, and pushed around by a bully who's younger than me." And my dad said, "No, actually, that's pretty much what it's like."

APRIL 26 [mood: oblivious]

My dad uses Head & Shoulders shampoo for his dandruff. Up until I was ten, I always thought Head & Shoulders was called that because it was a shampoo for both your head and back hair.

[mood: clean] APRIL 27

Here's something I don't understand about my school: all the soap dispensers have this weird pink Pepto Bismol–colored soap in them that smells a little like soap mixed with vomit. And I always wonder–why not just get normal soap? Is it that much cheaper to get the pink vomity kind?

I guess it could be worse. They could have those weird soap dispensers that squirt foam. Those are the worst. It's like someone put soap in their mouth and then spit it into your hand.

APRIL 28 [mood: traumatized]

I think that a good way to punish pickpockets is, instead of sentencing them to jail, just force them to wear tap shoes all the time.

[mood: confused] **APRIL 29**

I don't know why this is called a semicolon:

;

If a colon looks like this:

:

then a semicolon is half of that, or:

•

Right?

Ugh. I got a haircut earlier today, and now my neck's all itchy from the little hairs that fell down my shirt.

When the haircut was done, the barber did that thing where he held up a mirror behind me to show me what the back of my head looks like. I'm not sure why barbers do that. I don't care what the back of my head looks like. I'm not ever going to have to look at it. Still, I guess it's nice of them to show you that they didn't, like, shave a swearword into the back of your head or something while you weren't paying attention.

May

If you think about it, a box full of Alpha-Bits is just a bowl full of swearwords waiting to happen.

MAY 2 [mood: frustrated]

So I really like this girl in my homeroom, Chelsea Hamilton. She's the editor of the school newspaper, and really cool, and she looks sort of like Emma Stone, if Emma Stone were in the eighth grade. And I've been trying and trying to talk to her, but she doesn't even notice me. Like, literally, doesn't notice me. This morning, I said hi to her, and she said, "Oh, hi! Are you new? Did you just transfer to this school?" And I said, "No. We've gone to school together for the past seven years." And she said, "Ha-ha, very funny, I think I'd remember that. So, where did you transfer from?" And I said, "Ohio." It just seemed less embarrassing for both of us.

[mood: sleepy] MAY 3

This morning in homeroom, the captain of our wrestling team, Scott Scanlon, showed up with glasses—he said that he got them over the weekend. "My parents think I've never done so good in school 'cause I can't see the blackboard, so they sent me to an optimist to get my eyes checked, and now I can see more goodly." (I think that sentence may help to explain why I think Scott's eyesight isn't the reason he does poorly in school.)

Today in the lunchroom, I overheard Chelsea talking to her friends about Scott, and how much she liked his new glasses, because they make him look so smart and cute. Which gave me an idea: if they can make Scott look smart, I bet glasses would make me look like a genius!

Now I just need to figure out how to get myself some glasses. Ugh, I wish my eyesight were worse. Scott's so lucky to have crappy eyes.

So last night, I started trying to make my parents get me glasses. I told them I thought my eyesight was bad, and my mom said, "Well, what are you having trouble seeing?" And I said, "Everything." And my dad said, "It can't be everything. Are you nearsighted or farsighted? Are you having trouble seeing stuff that's close to you, like your textbooks? Or far away, like the TV?" And I said, "Which is the one where I can watch TV, but can't read my schoolbooks?" And he said, "That's farsighted." And I said, "That's what I am." My parents looked a little suspicious, but they made me an appointment with the eye doctor anyway.

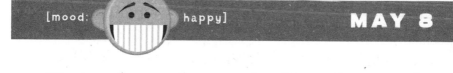

Went to the eye doctor today. He made me read the eye chart, and I was going pretty fast through it before I remembered that, if I wanted glasses, I had to pretend not to be able to read some of it. So I just stopped reading and said, "I can't see any of the rest of it." And he said, "Wait—you can't read anything else?" And I said, "Nope." And he said, "You were halfway through one of the lines. How could you read the first three letters, but not the next four?" And I said, "Lucky guess?"

Anyway, he started trying different lenses for each of my eyes, and each time, he'd say, "Better, worse, same?" And I was answering at random until he said, "A minute ago, you said that lens was better, and now you say it's worse." Which seemed uncool of him, to pull a trick question like that. But from then on out, I said every single lens was better than the one before it, until he finally said, "Well, these are the strongest lenses we have." And I said, "Awesome!" I bet Chelsea Hamilton will be really impressed when I tell her my prescription's *way* stronger than Scott's.

We picked up my new glasses today!

When I got home, I put them on, but I'm not sure how I look in them, because I can't see myself in the mirror when I'm wearing them. I showed them to Sophie, though, and she said, "Whoa! Cool!" And I said, "They look good?" And she said, "They make your eyes look so huge! You're like an anime character!" Which is probably good, right?

I wore my glasses to school for the first time today. I walked right up to Chelsea and said, "Hey, Chelsea! Notice anything different about me?" And she said, "I notice that you're late for class, but if you hurry, I won't write you up for it." And then I took my glasses off and discovered that the blurry thing I thought was Chelsea was actually Mrs. Plimpton, our vice principal. (And by the way: these are some pretty impressive glasses if they can make Mrs. Plimpton look like anything but Mrs. Plimpton.) As the morning went on, I also mistook our school janitor, a trash can, and a motivational poster of a kitten hanging from a branch for Chelsea.

NOT CHELSEA

NOT CHELSEA

HANG IN THERE

NOT CHELSEA

Finally, at lunch, Chuck pointed me in Chelsea's direction, and I walked over to say hi to her. And I was halfway there when I walked right into a sixth grader's tray full of sloppy joes. Man, they call those things "sloppy" for a reason—they kind of go everywhere.

Later in the day, my friend Kevin ran up to Chuck and me in the hallway and said, "Hey, did you hear? Some new kid from Ohio totally embarrassed himself in the cafeteria today! Hey—what happened to your shirt?"

Chelsea Hamilton and Scott Scanlon are officially dating now. Chuck tried to comfort me by saying, "Look, you did everything you could. But maybe it's not the glasses that Chelsea likes. Maybe it's the fact that he's got a huge neck and sort of looks like a professional wrestler. So you know . . . you never had a chance." I hate it when Chuck tries to comfort me.

To make things worse, I needed to figure out a way to explain to my parents that I won't be wearing my glasses anymore. So tonight at dinner, I announced that I didn't need my glasses anymore: "My vision's suddenly fine again! It's a miracle!" And my parents looked at me for a long moment, and then my dad said, "So what was her name?" And I said, "Chelsea." And he said, "Did it work?" And I said, "No." And he said, "Well, tell you what: it's a shame to let a nice, expensive pair of glasses like that go to waste. So how about you get a little more wear out of them—say, any time you want to watch TV for the next three weeks or so?"

So, if you'll excuse me, I should get going. A new *Big Bang Theory* is on, and I can't wait to hear it.

MAY 16 [mood: alarmed]

My school had a fire drill today. At two p.m., the fire-alarm bells sounded, and we all got into lines and walked single file out of the school. I've always thought the problem with fire drills is that they're nothing like a real fire—nothing's actually on fire, and nobody's choking on smoke or getting lost or anything. I think that to really test how ready the school is for a fire, they should blindfold everyone and put super-loud music on over the intercom and assign some students to just smack people at random as they try and fumble their way to the exit. It'd be better prepara-tion, and also a lot more fun.

WAK!

Today, the eighth grade took a trip to Liberty Falls Village. It's an educational theme park where people reenact what it was like to live in the 1780s, so everyone there is wearing an old-timey costume and doing old-timey stuff like churning butter or repairing carriage wheels or making candles. And you can ask them questions, and they have to answer in character as colonial people, which is less fun than it sounds, because once you've asked, "What're you doing?" and they say, "Churning butter," you kind of run out of things to talk about. After a little while, I started saying, "Hello! I am a visitor from the future! Look at my wristwatch—how do the digits on it keep changing? It's sorcery! Does it scare you?" until one guy in a blacksmith shop leaned over and said, "Dude, c'mon. This job sucks enough as it is."

And that's when I realized: this guy was only a couple of years older than me. He was probably a college student doing this for a summer job, and in a couple of years, I'll probably have a summer job that sucks just as much as his does. This wasn't just a field trip to our past. This was a trip to my future.

MAY 18 [mood: thoughtful]

When you say it out loud, the word *mailman* becomes redundant.

[mood: annoyed] **MAY 20**

A lot of my friends at school have joined a fantasy baseball league. Which sounds awesome—like, baseball games between dragons and sea serpents and wizards.

But it's not. It's about imagining baseball games between actual baseball players, using the statistics from their most recent games. So a lot of my friends' lunch-table conversation now is about comparing baseball statistics. It's basically like a really long, ongoing story problem in math class.

MAY 21 [mood: excited]

So this is almost the end of middle school—next week is final exams, and then I'm done!

We had an assembly this morning where Dr. Evans announced that, because this is the seventy-fifth anniversary of our school, our class will bury a time capsule in front of the school on Friday, to be opened in twenty-five years, so that kids in the future will know what life was like for us. "They did the same thing on the twenty-fifth and fiftieth anniversaries," she said. "So if anyone has anything they'd like to put in it, bring it to the ceremony tomorrow." Then she asked if anyone had any questions. I raised my hand and asked if we'd be digging up the time capsule that kids buried twenty-five years ago, and Dr. Evans kind of mumbled, "Actually, we don't know where it is. The people running the school back then forgot to write down where they put it. Are there any other questions?" And I raised my hand again and said, "Weren't you the one running the school twenty-five years ago?" And then she muttered something and dismissed the assembly.

Kevin, Chuck, and I spent all of lunchtime talking about what we'd put into the time capsule. Kevin suggested maybe we could put some pencils and erasers in there, but Chuck said he was pretty sure that pencils and erasers would still be around in twenty-five years. I finally decided that I'd bring in one of my comic books, because it'll probably be worth a lot of money in  twenty-five years, and all I need to do is show up when they dig it up and I can claim it.

MAY 22   [mood: thoughtful]

Toothpaste is a weird word, because it sounds like

you should use it to glue your teeth in. We should call denture adhesive *toothpaste*, and call toothpaste something else, like *mouthscrub*.

Tonight at dinner, my mom asked Sophie how school was today, and Sophie said it was great: "We played tag on the playground, and I won." And I said, "How do you win at tag?" And she said, "It's easy: when you're tagged, you don't chase anyone. You just sit down, and you wait. Sooner or later, the people who are playing the game will get tired of waiting for you to chase them, and they'll decide someone else is It." And my mom said, "So how does that mean you won?" And Sophie said, "Because you've bent them to your will. That means you're better than them."

I need to remember to be nice to Sophie, because I'm pretty sure that one day, I'm going to be working for her.

MAY 24　　　　　　　　　[mood: timely]

This morning we buried the time capsule at school. A bunch of people brought stuff to put in it—I put my comic book in it, and Chuck brought some of his old video-game cartridges that he doesn't use anymore, and Kevin brought a few erasers, and Doug Spivak brought a paper bag full of his old Pokemon cards, "so kids in the future will understand what we did for fun." Which was actually a pretty smart idea for Doug Spivak.

Anyway, they sealed it all up this morning and buried it. At lunch, I saw Doug Spivak sitting there, staring at an empty brown bag and a pile of Pokemon cards. I said, "I thought you put those in the time capsule." And he said, "So did I. I think I accidentally buried my lunch." And then he shrugged and said, "I hope kids still like tuna fish in twenty-five years."

If this blog is still around in a quarter century,

and any kids are reading it . . . sorry.

MAY 27 [mood: wistful]

I wish I had a fraternal twin, and that our last name was Identical, so we could be Identical twins who look nothing alike.

[mood: annoyed] MAY 29

So in history class today, we all had to pick a historical event to write a paper on. I chose the Alien and Sedition Acts, because they had *alien* in the name, but it turns out, they don't involve aliens at all. After school, I went to the library to check out some books for research, and the librarian said I wasn't allowed to, because I have an overdue Percy Jackson book from last November. It's really aggravating.

MAY 30 [mood: relieved]

Well, I had to tear apart my bedroom last night,

but I found my missing library book and brought it back to the library. The librarian said that I owed $49.70 in late fees on the book—"thirty-five cents a day for one hundred forty-two days." I said, "The book isn't even worth forty-nine seventy! The price on the back is just eight dollars." And she just shrugged and said, "Rules are rules." So I put the book back in my bag and said, "I lost the book. I'll pay to replace it."

And she said, "You didn't lose it. It's in your bag."

And I said, "Nope. It's lost."

And she stared at me for a long time.

And I stared back at her.

And finally, she sighed and said, "OK. That'll be eight dollars."

So I paid the fine. Then I said, "You know, if the library is missing a Percy Jackson book, I could sell you a replacement one." And she said, "Don't push your luck."

June

The fire extinguishers at our school are kept behind glass, like this:

IN CASE OF EMERGENCY BREAK GLASS

I'm not sure why. It seems like if there's an emergency, the last thing you want is a bunch of broken glass scattered everywhere.

You know that optical illusion where you're not supposed to know whether it's an image of two people talking, or a vase?

I figured out a third possibility: What if it's two people biting a vase?

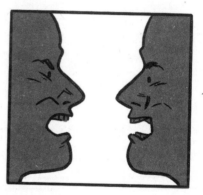

So my grandma Judy called this afternoon, and I picked up the phone. She asked to speak to my dad, and I told her that he wasn't home, but that she could talk to my mom. And she said, "No, that's fine. Just take a message: I'm coming to visit. A week from Friday. For three days." And I said, "Oh! If you get here on Thursday, you can come to my middle-school graduation." And she said, "Why on earth would I want to attend a middle-school graduation?"

Which, I had to admit, was actually a pretty good question.

Anyway, Sophie's pretty excited about the news, because she's Grandma Judy's favorite. And my mom just keeps muttering under her breath, "It's only three days, it's only three days," over and over and over again.

JUNE 4   [mood: tired]

Taking a break from studying for my final exams— tomorrow I have tests in math and science. Reading through my science textbook, I realized how much it must suck to be a scientist today, because all the easy stuff's already been discovered. Like, you know who was lucky? Sir Isaac Newton. Nowadays, scientists have to discover distant galaxies, or new elements, in order to become famous. But he was born at a time when you could become famous just for going, "Hey, you know what I discovered exists? Gravity. Gravity's mine. From here on out, I get credit for figuring that out."

JUNE 5   [mood: disgusted]

Ugh. Today was my math exam. I forgot my pencil, so I had to quickly borrow one, and without thinking, I asked Oliver Sloane, who sits across from me. As soon as he handed it over, I remembered: Oliver's a pencil chewer.

I don't think I did well on the exam, because all I could think the whole time was, I am holding something that has been in Oliver Sloane's mouth.

JUNE 6   [mood: thoughtful]

Almost done with exams—today was my English exam. I kind of wish I'd finished *To Kill a*

Mockingbird before the test, because I had to guess on a few questions. Does anyone out there know who Boo Radley is? I guessed that that was the name of a ghost, but I don't think that's right.

I just have history left to go. I've made flash cards with information on all the presidents. Looking through them, I don't know what's weirder: that all of our Founding Fathers wore wigs, or that they all chose

to wear the *same* wig. You'd think that at least one of them would've gone for a bright red one, or a beehive, or something.

JUNE 7   [mood: annoyed]

Ugh. Today was my last exam, in history, and I nearly got in trouble for cheating on it. During the test, Doug Spivak leaned over to me and whispered, "Tad! I need the names of the three ships Columbus took to America! I know one of them is the *Titanic*, but what are the other two?" And

I was whispering back that I couldn't help him when Mr. Campbell came over, picked up my test, and said, "Tad? If you're cheating on the test, I have to send you to the principal's office." And I said, "Mr. Campbell—if I were cheating, do you really think I'd cheat off of Doug Spivak?" He thought about it for a few seconds, and then said, "Good point," and handed my test back.

Anyway. That was my last exam—assuming I passed all of them, I'm done with middle school! I'm free! Woo-hooooooooooo!

JUNE 8 [mood: annoyed]

So today was my first day after completing middle school, and I was planning on celebrating by sleeping in and playing video games, but my mom woke me up this morning and said she needed my help in cleaning the house for Grandma Judy. So instead of enjoying my freedom, I wound up doing stupid stuff like scrubbing the bathroom sinks and helping my mom clean the refrigerator. We had to throw out some really gross stuff—some cheese with blue mold on it, a piece of lunch meat that had fallen in the back of the fridge and gotten crispy around the edges, and a giant bottle of ranch dressing that was almost completely full. When my mom saw it, she said, "I don't even know why we bought that. Nobody in the family even likes ranch dressing."

I didn't say a word.

JUNE 9 [mood: tired]

Today, Chuck's family went to Wombat World, the amusement park, and Chuck was allowed to bring one friend, so I went along. It was a lot of fun, especially since I'm now tall enough to go on all the rides, even the biggest and scariest roller coasters. Although to me, the scariest ride wasn't any of the giant roller coasters. It was the one shaped like a pirate ship that swings back and forth like a pendulum. Because after we were strapped in, right before the ride started, the ride operator said, "Spitting on this ride is strictly forbidden!" I don't even think it had occurred to anyone on the ride to do that. But now that he'd mentioned it, I spent the whole rest of the ride panicking that some kid sitting across from me would decide to try it.

It was crazy stressful.

Got in trouble with my mom today. I used the downstairs guest bathroom and washed my hands with the decorative soaps she'd put out for Grandma Judy, which are shaped like butterflies and seashells. And she said, "These are only for guests!"

I dunno. If I were a guest in someone's house and saw a bowl full of brand-new, untouched, never-been-used soaps, I'd kind of worry that no one in that house ever washed their hands.

[mood: relieved] **JUNE 13**

Tonight was my middle-school graduation. The ceremony was OK. They had it outside, on the athletic field at the school. And they began by giving out a whole bunch of awards to the graduating class, for being the best at English and math and science and everything. To me, the weirdest award was the one they gave out for perfect attendance—I feel like that's not really an achievement; all it means is that you never got sick. And to prove my point, the person who won it was Doug Spivak, who almost didn't come up to the stage, because they announced his name as "Douglas Spivak," and he forgot that Douglas was his full first name.

Our graduation speaker was the deputy mayor of our town, who told us that he wanted to talk to us about determination, and the power of positive thinking. And he talked for a little while about how, if you want something bad enough, you can make it happen through thinking about it positively. And just when it seemed like he was maybe going to wrap up, he said, "Now, let's get to the main part of my speech—what do I mean by being positive? Let's go through the word: *P*. What is *P* for?" And then he paused, and you could hear everyone in our class trying really hard not to laugh. And he said, "Persistence. *P* is for *persistence*. Let me talk a bit about persistence. . . ." And that's how he kept going—*O* is for *optimism*, *S* is for *strength*, and so on. By the time he got to *V*, I could see that everyone was getting sort of antsy—even the teachers up onstage were yawning and looking at their watches. And I started to think about how much I wanted the ceremony to be over, and I think everyone else did, too. And then, all of a sudden, a thunderstorm rolled in, and the whole ceremony got rained out. We all ran inside to the gym, and Dr. Evans announced that she would just send everyone their diplomas in the mail.

Maybe it was a coincidence, but I like to think

that the rainstorm came about because of the power of everyone's positive thinking.

Anyway, I'm now a middle-school graduate. I asked my dad if my eighth-grade diploma qualifies me to do anything. He shrugged and said, "Go to ninth grade, I guess."

So Grandma Judy arrived today. My dad and Sophie picked her up at the airport. She walked through the front door, looked around, and said to my mom, "I'm glad you didn't clean up for me. I'd hate to think I was a bother." Then she turned to me and said, "I didn't realize that's how boys were allowed to wear their hair these days." And then she went upstairs, so Sophie could help her unpack, and she could show her all the presents she'd brought for her. And I heard my mom mutter something under her breath about "it's just forty-eight hours, you can make it."

Ugh. Today was awful. Grandma Judy announced that she was going to take me and Sophie out "for a day of fun with my grandchildren." But since

Sophie's her favorite, that pretty much just meant that we spent the day doing stuff that Sophie and Grandma Judy enjoy. So we went to Dress Barn, Michaels arts-and-crafts store, the botanical gardens, and a store that sells doll furniture. The store that sells doll furniture was actually sort of fun, until Grandma Judy told me to stop pretending that I was a giant mutant lizard menacing a tiny city.

But that wasn't even the worst part of the day. The worst part was during dinner, when Grandma Judy announced, "So I actually came here to tell you all something. I have news. You remember that gentleman friend of mine, William? You all met him last summer?" And I started to ask, "Did he die?" when she said, "We're getting married! Wait—did you just ask if he died?" And I said, "No."

And then my dad said, "Mom—why do you have to get married? Can't you just be boyfriend and girlfriend?" And Grandma Judy said, "And live in sin?" And my dad said, "Dad wouldn't have wanted this." And she said, "Your father would understand. He would want me to be happy!" And my dad said, "No, he wouldn't!" And then neither of them said anything, and my mom said, "I'll go get our dessert!" and we all ate dessert so quietly that you could hear our forks scraping on our plates. It got so uncomfortable that I finally said twenty-one words I never in a million years thought I'd say: "I don't want the rest of my cake. I think I'm going to go help Sophie arrange her new doll furniture."

JUNE 16   [mood: glad]

So today was Grandma Judy's last day staying with us. By the time Sophie and I got up this morning, I guess she and my dad had talked some more, because he told us that we're going to Grandma Judy's wedding in August. And my mom said,

"And your father is very happy about that." And then there was a pause, and she turned to my dad and said, "Isn't that right, honey?" And my dad said, "Sure."

And then Grandma Judy said that she was glad to hear it, because she was really looking forward to having my dad walk her down the aisle, and Sophie being her flower girl. And then she turned to my mom and me and said, "And of course, you're invited, too." And my mom said, "Of course! Your wedding? In August? In Florida? I couldn't imagine a more fun time!"

JUNE 18 [mood: observant]

If it weren't already the name of a country, Finland would be a good name for a fish-themed amusement park.

So my parents are making me get a summer job again this summer, but I think I waited too long to start looking, because no one is hiring. I went down to the mall today and walked from store to store, but everyone kept telling me that they weren't even taking applications. By the thirtieth store, I wasn't even paying attention to where I was going—I'd just walk in, look for a salesperson, and ask, "Are you hiring?" Which got kind of awkward at one store, where the lady behind the counter stared at me and said, "Do you really think this is the place for you?" And then I realized I was in a lingerie store.

Which, it turns out, wasn't hiring.

My mom's car is getting repaired, so I went with my dad tonight to pick her up at the nursing home where she works. Here's a fun thing I learned while I was there: even if an old lady is wearing a T-shirt that says "Ask Me About My Grandchildren," you shouldn't ask her about her grandchildren, because she'll get sort of weirded out and alarmed by it and call security.

JUNE 23 [mood: excited]

Woo-hoo! Today I talked to Chuck, who said he found out that they're hiring caddies down at the golf course—so I called, and they offered to hire me! I have a summer job! There's a training session tomorrow, and then we can start caddying this weekend!

I'm very excited, even though my parents seem a little worried. My mom said, "Golf clubs are sort of heavy . . . ," and my dad said, "And golf courses are really big. . . ." But I figure that I don't have any problem carrying my backpack to and from school, and I like to walk around, so how bad could it be?

So yeah, I'm not going to be a caddy this summer. And neither is Chuck. The training session ended badly. Did you know that the reason golf clubs are called *woods* and *irons* is because they're made out of wood and iron? I would type more about it, but I'm kind of having trouble holding up my armss- ljskjfljksaedlkjdf sf

Today was really hot out, and I came up with a pretty good idea for a way to make money: I decided to open a lemonade stand. The only problem is, we didn't have any lemons in the house. You know how people say, "When life gives you lemons, make lemonade"? They never mention what to do when life doesn't give you lemons. I tried making orangeade, with orange juice, water, and sugar, but it just tasted weird and wrong. And then I saw that we had some milk and some chocolate syrup, so I opened a chocolate-milk stand. But I realized pretty quickly that nobody really wants to buy chocolate milk that's been sitting out in the sun for a while—and changing the name to "hot chocolate" seemed like it might help, but it turns out, nobody wants hot chocolate in the middle of June. After all that, I only wound up making $3 from one of our neighbors, who pretended to sip from the cup and said, "I'm going to take this back inside and finish it later."

JUNE 27 [mood: psyched]

So tonight, my mom said that she might have a job opportunity for me. She said, "You know Mrs. Wagner? From down the street?" And I said, "Yeah . . ."

And my mom said, "She needs a babysitter this Saturday night." And I said, "Isn't she a bit old to have a babysitter?" And my mom said, "You know what I mean. She needs someone to watch Kyle." Kyle's her son, who's eight. From the sound of things, she just needs someone to give him dinner, hang out with him for an hour or so, and then make sure he goes to bed, and wait for Mrs. Wagner and her husband to come home. So I said, "Sure." And my mom said, "You know, I made a lot of money babysitting when I was your age. If you do a good job at the Wagners', tell them to recommend you to their friends. Maybe this'll be how you earn money this summer!" And I said, "So I can get paid to watch other kids?" And my mom said, "Sure! It's a valuable service!" And I said, "Can I get paid every time you make me hang out with Sophie?" And she said, "Absolutely not."

It was worth a try.

JUNE 28   [mood: more psyched]

The more I think about it, the more excited I am about the idea of making money by babysitting. I need to make a good impression so the Wagners recommend me to all of their friends, so I've been thinking about ways to entertain Kyle. I'm going to bring over some decks of cards, and a board game, and maybe a jigsaw puzzle, so we'll have plenty of options to have fun.

JUNE 29 [mood: happy]

9:44 p.m.

So I'm at the Wagners' house right now. (I'm on Mr. Wagner's computer, in his office—he said I could use it if I wanted to, so long as I didn't click on his browser history or open any files.)

Tonight went OK: I showed up at seven thirty with all the stuff to entertain Kyle, and Mrs. Wagner said, "I'm glad you brought a five-hundred-piece puzzle, but you know he's going to go to bed in an hour and a half, right?"

Anyway, it turned out Kyle didn't want to play board games or anything—he just wanted to watch TV. So we hung out and we watched some *Scooby-Doo*, and then it was his bedtime, so he brushed his teeth and put on his pajamas and went to bed.

(Speaking of *Scooby-Doo*: How is it that, in every episode, Fred and Daphne and Velma figure out that weird, unexplained phenomena are being caused by men wearing rubber masks, but none of them have ever thought to check if their talking, crime-solving Great Dane is just a guy in a dog suit?)

AWKWARD...

So, now I'm just hanging out, waiting for the Wagners to come home. They even said I could eat a Popsicle from the freezer! This is the easiest money I've ever made!

10:04 p.m.

If anyone out there knows how to get a grape Popsicle stain out of a white couch, can you email me right away?

11:44 p.m.

I don't even want to get into it, but let's just say: I have managed to wind up in debt as a result of babysitting. I need to make quite a bit of money now. And I will not be able to make it back by babysitting for the Wagners.

July

[mood: itchy]

Arrrrrrrgh. I was hanging out on our porch tonight with our family, and when we came inside, I discovered that I was covered with mosquito bites. Stupid mosquitos. I've been thinking about it, and I've got a great solution to prevent mosquito bites. They bite us in order to drink our blood, right? Well, why not fill up a hummingbird feeder with blood, and let the mosquitos drink it from there? That way, they get all the blood they want, and none of us gets bitten.

I told my mom about my brilliant idea, and even

showed her my diagram. She said it was the most disgusting idea she'd ever heard. "But we wouldn't get bitten by mosquitos!" I said. And she said, "You also could just put on the insect repellent like I kept telling you to."

BEFORE AFTER!

It sucks to be a brilliant inventor and have nobody else realize it.

JULY 4 [mood: tired]

Today our whole family went to the park for the big Fourth of July celebration our town has each year. It was OK—they had games, and a bunch of clowns, and three mimes. (Originally, we thought there were four mimes, but it turned out one of them was just a crazy person who thought he was trapped in a glass box.) They also had stands where you could buy helium balloons. I don't understand why anyone sells helium balloons— we must've seen something like twenty little kids crying because they'd let go of their balloon, or it had popped, or they were fighting with their brother or sister over it. Buying a kid a helium balloon is like paying $3 to guarantee that someone will be crying sometime in half an hour.

JULY 5 [mood: happy]

I got a job! I got a job! I got hired down at the Smart Mart grocery store as a bagger! I went there with my mom tonight, and she saw them putting up a "Help Wanted" sign, and she took me to the manager, a woman named Lisa, and said, "If you're hiring, he's available!" And before I knew it, I'd filled out a form and been given a time card and was told to come back tomorrow at nine.

Today was my first day on the job at Smart Mart. Lisa was really nice—she gave me an apron and a time card and a name tag, and showed me around, and she gave me a quick talk about how to bag groceries. But then I was out there, actually doing it, and it was really stressful, because the job's a lot more complicated than it seems. There are a lot of things you should never do as a grocery bagger. Like, you should never put all the canned items in one bag, because it'll make the bag impossible to lift. And you should never put a carton of eggs below a watermelon.

And even if someone is buying a really, really large amount of toilet paper, don't say to them, "Wow! You buy a lot of toilet paper!" because it makes everything awkward for both of you.

The other baggers said I did an OK job for my first day, but that I was lucky that Lisa was the manager on duty, and not Mr. Nelson. I asked why, and they said, "You'll see."

JULY 7 [mood: annoyed]

Today was my second day of bagging groceries, and now I know what the other baggers meant about Mr. Nelson. I met him first thing in the morning, when I came in—I went to punch in my time card, and he was standing next to it, looking at his watch. I guess it was 9:02 a.m., and I was supposed to get there at nine. He took me into his office and gave me a long speech about how, if I'm late, I'm letting the whole Smart Mart team down, and how a chain is only as strong as its weakest link, and how there's no *I* in *team*. Which seems like kind of a weird saying, because the letters for *me* are in *team*.

Plus, there are plenty of words that mean *team* that *do* have an *I* in them, like *unit* and *organization*.

And there's no *I* in *eye*, even though they're pronounced the same.

And there's an *I* in *giraffe*, but that doesn't mean that every giraffe has a person inside of it.

But I didn't point any of that out to Mr. Nelson. I also didn't point out that, if me being two minutes late was a huge burden to everyone else, then him taking twenty minutes to lecture me on lateness was probably ten times more of a burden. I just nodded and went to work.

JULY 8 [mood: frustrated]

Grrrrr.

Today, I made a special effort to arrive at the store early, so I wouldn't get in trouble again with Mr. Nelson. And I actually got there at 8:54, and punched in. And about an hour later, I was bagging groceries when he came over and asked to see me in his office. At first, I thought he was going to tell me how happy he was that I'd gotten there early, but instead, he lectured me for a while about how I can't punch in before my shift starts, because then I'm getting paid for time that I'm not supposed to be here, which is stealing from the company. And he talked about how it doesn't feel like I'm a team player, and he really needs me to be giving 110 percent to the store. Which is funny, because what I'd done was give him 10 percent more of an hour than I was supposed to. But before I could point that out, he'd taken out my time card and changed my punch-in time to nine, and then made me initial the change.

JULY 9 [mood: thoughtful]

I wonder if fish remember the story of Noah's Ark as "the time God got mad at everyone but us."

[mood: thirsty] JULY 10

If your last name is Pepper, I bet you think twice before becoming a doctor.

JULY 11 [mood: tired]

Back to work at the Smart Mart. Lisa was the

manager on duty, so it was pretty relaxed. There was one weird moment when I had just finished bagging two big boxes of wine, a tube of hemorrhoid cream, and a lot of Lean Cuisine single-serve dinners, and looked up and saw that the person buying them was Mr. Swanson, my middle-school guidance counselor. I looked at him, he looked at me, and then we both looked away as he picked up his bags and left. Afterward, the cashier, Bev, leaned over and said, "Do you know that guy? He comes in here every week and buys the same stuff every single time."

JULY 13 [mood: awkward]

Today at the store, I worked with Bev as the cashier again. We were having a lot of fun, because under her breath, she was pointing out all the people who are regular customers. There's the Cat Lady, who

buys twenty cans of cat food every single week. And Banana Guy, who buys a single banana every afternoon. And Mr. Exact Change, who always holds up the line by insisting on paying for everything with exact change down to the penny.

And then Bev said, "Oh! Here comes the Crazy Coupon Lady!" And I looked up, all ready to see some crazy-looking woman, and realized: it's my mom. And before I could say anything, my mom came over to our register and said, "Hi, honey! I got us hot dogs for dinner!" And then she turned to Bev and said, "I hope my son isn't giving you too much trouble here. Now, let me see, I have a coupon for the hot dogs, and this cereal, and the tuna fish, and the canned soup . . ." And Bev got really embarrassed, and we kind of didn't talk to each other very much for the rest of my shift.

JULY 15 [mood: annoyed]

Tonight at dinner, my mom asked me, "Tad, are you working next Saturday?" And without thinking, I said, "No, I have this Saturday off." And she said, "Great! You can help me out with the baby shower!"

I have to learn to always think before answering my mom's questions. She's super tricky sometimes.

Anyway, I guess my mom's agreed to have a baby shower for her friend Julie, from her book club. I'm not sure I've ever even met Julie—whenever my mom's book club comes over, my dad usually takes me to the movies, so that neither of us has to be around for it. But now both of us are going to be stuck helping out with the baby shower. I asked my dad what a baby shower was—he said it's a party where women open up one box after another with tiny outfits in them and say how cute they are. I asked how long they usually take, and he said, "Around five hours." I said, "You're kidding." He said, "Nope."

JULY 16 [mood: annoyed]

Today, Mr. Nelson took me off of grocery-bagging duty and made me spray down all the grocery conveyor belts.

And then, once I was done, he went around and inspected them and made me do it a second time, because they weren't clean enough. He told me he wanted them all to be "as clean as a whistle," which is weird, because whistles are full of dried spit.

JULY 18 [mood: happy]

A good day at work: I was on the express lane, for people with ten items or less, which made every bag much quicker and easier to pack. The only exception was when one guy came through the lane with, like, twenty items. Bev tried to point out to him that he couldn't go through the line with that many items, but he was on his cell phone and just snapped his fingers at her and said, "Ring it all up quick; I'm in a hurry."

Since he was in such a hurry, I decided I should pack his bag quickly, so I put his lightbulbs, bread, and pie at the bottom of a bag, threw his gallon of milk and a bag of kitty litter on top, handed them to him, and told him to have a nice day.

Today, I was off work, and so my mom and I went to the party store to get plates and streamers for her friend Julie's baby shower. I'd never been in a party store before. I'd always thought it would be kind of a fun place, what with the word *party* right in the name, but all the workers there looked really depressed, like there'd been some horrible accident the day before where one of their coworkers had drowned in a vat of confetti.

All the baby-shower decorations had pictures like this on them:

Sophie asked why, and I told her it was because storks used to sneak into maternity wards and steal babies; we put

these pictures on maternity stuff in order to commemorate all the babies that were eaten by birds, in the days before stork-proofing.

My dad and I went to BuyBuy Baby tonight to get some baby stuff for the shower. BuyBuy Baby is not a good name for a store. It sounds like it's either a place you would go to buy a baby, a store where babies can shop, or a place to go to say good-bye to a baby. Like some kind of baby airport or something.

I just got out of helping my mom with the baby shower! It had barely started, and guests were still arriving, and my mom sent me out to offer every-one sandwiches. And when I was serving them, I said, "Congratulations, Julie! I bet you can't wait for the baby to get here!" And the woman I was serving said, "I'm not Julie." And I said, "Sorry. I just assumed, 'cause you're pregnant." And she said, "No, I'm not."

And then my mom came over and said, "Thanks, Tad. I'll handle everything from here." And she sent me to my room for the rest of the party.

So, for future reference: saying one of her friends looks pregnant = surefire way to get out of helping out at my mom's parties. I'm going to have to remember that.

JULY 22 [mood: annoyed]

I think if I had to choose one thing I hate the most about working at my summer job, it'd be a tie between getting lectured on teamwork by Mr. Nelson and having to listen to the same ten stupid songs that play on a loop in the store all day long. By the two hundredth time you hear it, Rick Astley's "Never Gonna Give You Up" sounds less like a promise, and more like a threat.

[mood: crafty] **JULY 23**

I went over to Chuck's house today and we spent a while playing *Minecraft*. It's an online game where you're a warrior who's dropped into the wilderness, and you can gather bricks and stones and build a house for yourself. Chuck and I spent the last few days building a pretty awesome castle with a moat, and torches, and a drawbridge. I showed it to my mom tonight, and she said, "Oh! Neat! It's like a dollhouse!" And I said, "No, it's not like a dollhouse. I'm a warrior." And she said, "It sort of seems like a dollhouse." And I said, "It's not a dollhouse! I have a sword!" And she said, "Fine. It's not a doll-house. It's just a house that you built and furnished, that an imaginary person lives in, that you like to play with." Exactly. I don't know why that was so hard for her to understand.

JULY 24   [mood: bored]

My dad is watching a golf tournament on TV. I'm not sure why. Golf is the only sport that's so boring, I'm surprised people don't actually fall asleep while playing it.

I think my work at the store is getting to me. Last night, I dreamed that I was standing at the end of a giant conveyer belt, and groceries kept coming toward me on it, faster and faster, and I had to keep bagging them. And then it wasn't just groceries—it was scary stuff, like sharks and lions and chain saws. And the weirdest part was, in the dream, all I could think was, Do I put the sharks on the bottom of the bag? Or the top?

Rough day at the Smart Mart. Mr. Nelson fired one of the baggers, Eddie, for being five minutes late. Eddie was kind of upset about it—he went into Mr. Nelson's office and changed the music that plays over the store's loudspeakers, then locked the door. So for an hour, the music that played in the store was loud death metal. It was kind of a nice break from Rick Astley, actually.

Today was an even worse day at the store. Mr. Nelson fired two clerks and a guy who worked at the deli case for being late. He told us all that "their tardiness wasn't fair to the rest of you." And then he told us that, until they hired more baggers, we'd all have to work longer hours and extra shifts. Which didn't seem especially fair to any of us, but nobody said anything, because Mr. Nelson seemed like he might fire one of us next.

So today I went to Mr. Nelson and reminded him that I couldn't work next week, because I'm going to Florida for Grandma Judy's wedding. And he said, "I'm sorry, but I need you to come in." And I told him that I actually got permission to take those days off way back when I was hired, and he said, "Look, Tad, we're running short on staff right now. It's crunch time, so I need you to step up to the plate, hit the ground running, and take one for the team." And I said, "You know how you always say there's no *I* in *team*?" And he said, "Yeah." And I said, "Well, there are two in 'I quit.'" And then I left.

It's weird that the whole plot of *Cinderella* kind of hinges on the idea that no two people can have the same shoe size.

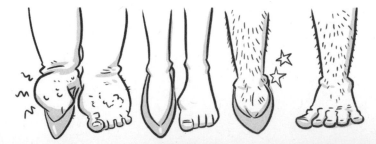

Well, in two days, we're flying down to Florida for Grandma Judy's wedding. My mom took me to the Smart Mart tonight to get some travel-size toothpaste, and we wound up going through Bev's checkout line. I looked down the row and saw that Mr. Nelson was bagging groceries at another register. He seemed really worn-out and tired. Bev leaned over and said, "After you quit, two more baggers left, too. He's had to bag groceries himself ever since."

I felt a little bad for him. But not very.

August

[mood: proud]

Tomorrow morning, we're going to Florida for Grandma Judy's wedding. My mom's been really stressed about it, so I tried to help out as much as I could. For instance, I packed my own suitcase, and when I realized I didn't have enough clean socks for the trip, I did a load of laundry for myself.

I also threw my

suit in there—it smelled a little musty because I haven't worn it since my great-aunt Sophie's funeral last year.

It was a little wrinkly coming out of the dryer, but I'm sure if I hang it up in Florida, it'll be fine.

I bet my mom'll be really impressed with how self-sufficient I am.

AUGUST 2 [mood: tired]

So we flew down to Florida this morning. I got in trouble on the airplane because I was playing on my GamePort XL with my headphones on, and didn't hear them telling us to shut off all our electronic devices. The flight attendant came over and said, "You need to shut that off! It's very dangerous to have it on

during takeoff!" And all I could think is, If it's so dangerous, why on earth would you ever let someone bring one of these on a plane?

It's nice to be here, though. We drove past a lot of restaurants with signs for "Early Bird Specials," which is a weird thing for a restaurant to advertise, because the main thing I know about an early bird is, it eats a worm.

Anyway, we stopped by Grandma Judy's retirement home to say hello, and she seemed really happy to see us. Her fiancé, William, was there, and some of his family, and Grandma Judy pointed to one little girl and said to Sophie, "William has a granddaughter, too! She's four years old, and her name is Rose, and she's *also* going to be a flower girl!" And Sophie said, "What do you mean? You can't have two flower girls!" And Grandma Judy said, "Of course you can! And won't it be fun to share?" And Sophie looked at Rose and mumbled, "She's much cuter than me. No one's even gonna notice me." And then she didn't talk for the rest of the afternoon. I realized after a little while that she was giving Grandma Judy the silent treatment, but Grandma Judy was too busy talking about her wedding planning to notice. It was actually kind of nice.

AUGUST 3 [mood: annoyed]

Well, this morning, Sophie woke up in a better mood than she was in yesterday. She came down to breakfast and said, "I shouldn't be complaining so much. Tomorrow is Grandma Judy's day, and I just want her to be happy." And my mom said, "That's really sweet. You should tell her that." And Sophie said, "Besides, Grandma Judy doesn't have that many days left." And my mom said, "Leave out that last part."

Meanwhile, the rest of my dad's side of the family arrived for the wedding. My uncle Kevin and his partner Steven drove in together around lunchtime, and my aunt Stacy showed up tonight with my cousins Scott, Derek, and Rick. I don't like my cousins—they're triplets, and sixteen, and have buzz cuts, and are kind of jerks. (A few years ago, they came to visit us, and they sneaked into my room when I was sleeping and wrote *BUTT* on my face. Which would be bad enough, but they used permanent marker, and it wouldn't come off. So I added *ON* to it, so it said *BUTTON*. It didn't make sense, but I figured it was better to walk around with *BUTTON* on my head than *BUTT*.)

Anyway, I was hoping they'd forgotten, but the first thing they said when they saw me was, "Hey, Buttonhead!"

I hate them so much.

Today was Grandma Judy's wedding. It got off to a pretty lousy start: I put on my suit for the wedding, and it didn't really fit right.

Sophie saw me try it on, and she said, "You look like a sausage." Which was sort of true.

And my mom said, "What did you do to your suit?" And I said, "Nothing! All I did was wash it!" And she sort of turned white and said, "You washed a wool suit?" And before I could answer, she just sighed and said, "Well, we don't have time to get you a new suit. Go put on another pair of pants, at least, and we'll go to the wedding." And I said, "But I don't have another pair of pants. All I brought were shorts." And my mom looked at my dad, and he said, "Um, yeah, me too." And my mom said, "Am I the only one who brought more than one pair of pants on this trip?"

So that's how I wound up going to my grandmother's wedding wearing a pair of my mom's pants. They were tan, and made out of a silky material, and they didn't have any pockets and fit sort of funny. I complained, but my mom said, "Honey, no one will even notice. From a distance, they look just like men's pants."

And I believed her. Right up until I walked into the wedding and one of my cousins shouted, "Hey! Buttonhead's wearing ladypants!" And then they all high-fived.

They called me "Ladypants" for the rest of the day. I miss "Buttonhead" already.

Aside from that, it was a very nice wedding. Sophie did a good job as the flower girl, although she did seem to throw a lot of the petals directly into Rose's face.

At the end of the night, we looked over and saw Grandma Judy, dancing cheek-to-cheek with

William. They looked really happy—even my mom thought so. She turned to my dad and said, "Wow. I don't think I've ever seen her this happy." And my dad said, "Yeah. It's sweet, isn't it?" And then we went over to say good night, and we realized that they weren't dancing cheek-to-cheek—Grandma Judy was whispering in William's ear that he was dancing terribly, and that he should just let her lead. And my mom said, "OK, yeah, that's more like it." And my dad said, "Yup."

AUGUST 5 [mood: happy]

We're finally home from Florida. I'm glad to be home—it wasn't a fun trip back. I couldn't play on my Game-Port, because the woman next to me was a very nervous flyer, and she was grabbing on to my hand for the whole flight.

I think it's weird that there aren't any holidays in August. Every other month has at least one, and February has three, probably because February sucks so much that's the only way to get through it. It's like, "Hey, it's cold and dark and depressing, but here's a groundhog! And presidents! And valentines!"

If I ever get to have a holiday named after myself, I'm going to have it happen in August. I know that usually, a holiday goes near the birthday of whoever it's honoring, and my birthday's in March. But I'm going to call it "Tad's Birthday (Observed)."

So that's settled. Now I just need to do something that's worth getting a holiday named after me.

The Summer Olympics are on right now. My dad and I just spent an hour watching a shot-put competition. The Olympics are weird—it's like, for two weeks every four years, everyone in the country has this mass delusion that stuff like track-and-field is really, really interesting, and then we all recover and go back to normal.

Still, I did figure out something that'd make me far more likely to watch shot-put competitions: What if, instead of *throwing* a sixteen-pound metal ball with their bare hands, the competitors had to *catch* one with their bare hands? I'd watch that any day of the week.

AUGUST 9 [mood: eager]

Awesome news! The people who live behind us, the Warrens, are going on vacation for the weekend, and they hired me to watch their dog, Virginia Woof! I just have to go over and feed her and take her for a walk every day, and they'll pay me $20!

Bad news: I took Virginia Woof for her first walk today, and a police officer stopped me and told me I had to curb my dog. And I said, "You mean, like, walk her along the curb? That seems dangerous." And he said, "No. I mean you have to pick up her poop." And I said, "With my bare hands?" And he said, "No. You should have a plastic bag with you, or a newspaper, or something." And I said, "Oh. I don't have anything with me." And he handed me a piece of paper, which seemed nice of him, until I realized it was a ticket for not picking up the dog's poop. It's a $25 ticket. So I'm going to lose money on this whole dog-sitting thing.

Plus, apparently, I'm going to need to handle poop, which is just gross.

AUGUST 13 [mood: thoughtful]

If you think about it, firemen shouldn't be called *firemen*. Arsonists should be called *firemen*. Firemen should be called *antifiremen* or *water-men* or *fire-spraying-with-a-hose-guys*.

[mood: worried] AUGUST 15

So today, my family had a cookout on the patio. And my burger was kind of burned and I pointed it out as nicely as I could by saying, "Are you sure this isn't just a piece of charcoal?" And at the same time, Sophie was poking at her potato salad, and said, "I'm trying to find the potatoes in all this mayonnaise. It's like a ghost had diarrhea."

And my mom and dad both looked at us, and my mom said,

"Well, your dad and I worked really hard to make dinner tonight, but I guess it's not up to your standards. So, tell you what: for the next week, you two are in charge of cooking dinner." And Sophie said, "What?" And I said, "But we're on vacation!" And my mom said, "Well, great! That means you'll have plenty of time to plan menus and cook. I'll take you to the store tomorrow, and starting Monday, you two can cook for the whole week." And then she went back into the kitchen to get the brownies she'd made for dessert. Which were a little dry, but it didn't seem like a good time to mention that.

Anyway, I think my parents are trying to show us that it's harder than it looks, but I bet Sophie and I can prove them wrong. I've gone online and found a bunch of recipes—we're gonna have an awesome week of dinners.

AUGUST 16 [mood: hungry]

So tonight, Sophie and I made dinner for the first time, and we learned a lot. For instance: Did you know that a chicken's heart and liver and neck are called giblets?

And that if you buy a whole chicken, the giblets can be found in a plastic bag inside the chicken?

And that if you roast the chicken without removing the giblets, you'll find a mess of melted plastic and chicken organs inside it when you cut it open?

And that if that happens, your parents will insist that you throw the chicken away?

And that even if they made you throw the chicken away, your parents might still insist that cooking dinner is your responsibility?

And that if you can't find anything else to cook, your whole family might wind up having PB&J sandwiches for dinner?

Well, they are, they can, it will, they did, they might, and we did.

AUGUST 17 [mood: nauseated]

Tonight, Sophie and I tried making spaghetti and meatballs. But we both found handling the ground meat kind of gross, and we didn't have a lot of time, so Sophie said, "Instead of making lots of little meatballs, why don't we just make four big ones, one for each of us?" Which seemed like a really good idea, right up until we served dinner and discovered that big meatballs don't cook all the way through, so every meatball was raw in the middle.

Meatball Cross Section Fig.1

They were like Everlasting Gobstoppers of salmonella. Anyway. We had PB&J again.

AUGUST 18 [mood: thirsty]

Every day, I learn something new about cooking. Apparently, when a recipe says "two tsp salt," that means two teaspoons, and not two tablespoons.

Tried making something simple: soup. Didn't put the lid on the blender right. Spent most of tonight scrubbing butternut squash off the kitchen walls. We're running low on PB&J now.

AUGUST 20 [mood: amazed]

So tonight, Sophie and I made cheeseburgers. And they looked awesome, right up until I realized she'd accidentally left the plastic wrapping on the cheese slices. My parents came outside and saw the plastic-covered burgers, and my mom said, "That's it. I give up. I can't eat PB and J again." And my dad called for a pizza, and my mom said, "I hope you kids have learned your lesson from this." And Sophie said, "What lesson was this supposed to teach us?" And my mom said, "I don't even remember. But I hope you learned it, because I don't want to ever go through another week like this one."

They say that whatever doesn't kill you makes you stronger, but that doesn't seem right, because wouldn't elderly people—the people who've gone the longest without being killed—be crazy super strong?

It's weird that, if you leave a grape out in the sun for long enough, it'll turn into a raisin, but if you leave a banana out in the sun, all that'll happen is it'll become a brown, sticky mess and your dad will yell at you for attracting ants to the back patio.

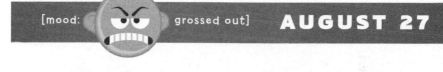

AUGUST 26 [mood: in trouble]

My mom's mad at Sophie and me. We all got kicked out of Bed Bath & Beyond today, but it's not really our fault. The sign very clearly said "Throw Pillows."

[mood: grossed out] AUGUST 27

I was watching a TV special today about astronauts, and now all I can think about is how disgusting it would be to have a runny nose in zero gravity.

If you study the planet Uranus, you probably never tell people what you study without putting the words *the planet* in front of it.

I bet that when elephants laugh so hard that water comes out of their nose, it's no big deal.

September

Today my mom took me and Sophie to the store to stock up on school supplies. For geometry, I needed to get a compass, which isn't what you'd think. It's not one of those round pocket watch–looking things you use to figure out which direction is north. It's this weird two-pronged pointy thing that you use to draw circles. I don't get why both these things are called *compasses*. Like, there should be enough words in the English language that two

Northfinder!

Circlemaker!

completely different things shouldn't have to share one. That's why I'm starting a movement to call each of them by a different name.

Today's Labor Day. I asked my parents what the day is supposed to celebrate, and my mom told me it's a salute to the labor movement, which fought for stuff like the eight-hour day and the five-day workweek. I told her that in honor of the labor movement, I wouldn't be setting the table tonight. My mom said that if that was the case, she'd salute the labor movement by not making dinner tonight. And my dad said that he'd do his part by not driving us to the movies after dinner. So I said, "Fine, I'll set the table." And my dad said, "Congratulations. Now you understand how strikes get resolved."

Today was my first day of high school, and for

the most part, it was fine—it was a lot like middle school, only bigger.

There was one small screwup with my class schedule, though: instead of being placed in Spanish Level II, I was put in Honors Level German. I tried to tell the teacher that I was in the wrong class, but she insisted that students were to speak only German in her classroom, and since I didn't know how to say "I don't know how to speak German" in German, I just had to sit there for the whole class. I'm not sure exactly what the subject of the class was—it was either irregular verbs, or how to clear phlegm from the back of your throat.

Kein Englisch!

Other than that, the teachers all seem pretty cool, and even the older kids seem fine. I'd heard that seniors pick on freshmen, but the ones that I met were super helpful. Some of them even sold Chuck and me passes to the school's swimming pool at half-price, which was really nice of them. They said that the pool's right behind the gym, so tomorrow, Chuck and I are going to bring our trunks in and go swimming during lunch.

SEPTEMBER 4 [mood: depressed]

Found out today that not only does the school not sell swimming-pool passes, it doesn't even have a swimming pool. It's bad enough that those seniors lied to us and took our money—I just really wish that we'd figured it out before we walked into the gym in our bathing suits during the girls' volleyball team practice.

So far, high school's been going pretty well, except for one thing: my locker is a bottom locker. And even worse, it's below Beth Carmichael's. She's super popular, so all of her friends cluster around her between classes to hang out and talk—which makes it impossible for me to get to my locker. Today I had to wait until the bell rang, just to get my Spanish workbook. I tried to explain that I was only late because Beth and her friends couldn't decide whether she should trim her bangs or not, but I still got marked as tardy.

OK, this locker situation is getting bad. Today, I tried to get into my locker to get my geometry book, and Beth's friend Jessica glared at me and said, "Ex-CUSE me. We're having a PRIVATE CONVERSATION." And then she rolled her eyes and went back to talking to Beth. So I wound up being late to geometry—if I get one more tardy notice, then I have an automatic detention.

Next week, I think I'm just going to try carrying all my books around with me.

SEPTEMBER 7 [mood: rested]

Today's Saturday. Spent the day celebrating the fact that I don't have to deal with Beth for two whole days by sitting on the couch, watching TV, and eating Teddy Grahams.

I bet that somewhere out there, there's some guy named Theodore Graham whose life got ruined by the invention of Teddy Grahams.

LET'S SEE HOW THE COOKIE CRUMBLES, TEDDY!

DON'T BITE OFF MORE THAN YOU CAN CHEW!

T. GRAHAM

OK. I'm never carrying all my books around with me again. My backpack got super heavy, and by fifth period, I was hunched over, just trying to get to my next class. Chuck saw me and said, "Man. You look like a sad turtle." I tried to go put some books back in my locker, but Beth and all her friends were gathered around, trying to help her decide which lip gloss matched her Trapper Keeper better. It's going to be a long year.

Ugh. The problem is even worse than I thought. Today, I went up to Beth at lunch and said, "I think we need to figure out a system for us to get our books between classes." And she said, "I'm sorry. Who are you?" It's not even that she doesn't care about me—*she's had the locker above mine for a week, and doesn't even know who I am.* It's like I'm invisible or something. This must be how Bruce Willis felt at the end of *The Sixth Sense*.

So today at lunch, Kevin and Chuck and I tried to figure out a solution for the Beth problem. Kevin suggested that maybe if I put a sardine in my locker, it would smell so bad that Beth's friends wouldn't want to hang out there anymore. And Chuck said, "Wouldn't that make Tad's stuff smell all sardine-y, too?" And Kevin said, "Oh, yeah. Right. I forgot about that."

We agreed that I have no options—Chuck said that he hasn't seen a girl be that mean to me since the time I asked Heather Blankenship to the school dance.

Wait a minute.

I just had an idea. I think I've figured out how to get my locker back.

So this morning, first thing before school, I went up to Beth Carmichael and all her friends as they were standing around our lockers. And I said,

"Hi, Beth. I'm Tad. I just want you to know that I really, really like you, and I want us to go out. Do you want to go to homecoming with me?" She got this really upset look on her face, and backed away slowly, and all of her friends followed her. And for the rest of the day, every time I went to get my stuff out of my locker, she'd see me, look really nervous, and hurry away. By the end of the

day, she and her friends had started hanging out near Jessica's locker, all the way at the other end of the hall. I told Chuck about it, and he said, "You know, repelling girls is a pretty lousy superpower. But every once in a while, it does come in handy."

I read today that if you put an infinite number of monkeys at an infinite number of typewriters, sooner or later, one of them would type the complete works of William Shakespeare. Which is kind of amazing to think about. But it's weirder still to realize that there'd also be a monkey who'd type the complete works of William Shakespeare, but with exactly one typo. And a monkey who'd type this exact blog entry.

I don't get how you could kill two birds with one stone. Is it like a ricochet thing?

We had an assembly today where the lieutenant governor spoke. She came to talk to us about her job and how important it is to get involved in politics, and then she took questions from us. One kid raised his hand and asked if she could get us better school lunches, and she said that that wasn't her department. Another kid asked if she could get us less homework, and she said that she couldn't really do that, either. And then my friend Kevin raised his hand and asked, "What does a lieutenant governor do?" and she said that she assists the governor. And he said, "Like how?" And she said, "Well, I handle a lot of things on his agenda." And Kevin said, "Name three things you handle." And she said, "I handle so many things, I can't just name three." And Kevin said, "You don't actually do anything, do you?" And then she said that she needed to go someplace else to do important lieutenant-governor things, and Kevin got detention.

SEPTEMBER 17 [mood: amused]

In biology class today, Mr. Perkins explained to us that everything in the world is connected to everything else, and told us about something called "the butterfly effect": "It's possible that a butterfly flapping its wings in China could cause a tidal wave in Latin America." Doug Spivak raised his hand and asked, "So why haven't we killed all of them?" And Mr. Perkins said, "Killed who?" And Doug said, "All the Chinese butterflies. It seems, like, better safe than sorry, right?"

I bet that if anteaters ever learned to talk, they'd be really hurt that we call them anteaters.

I don't know what this symbol on my keyboard is for:

\#

Is it maybe in case you want to play a really tiny game of tic-tac-toe?

Today, these signs went up all over the school:

Our high-school team is the Lakeville Sharks. I'm not sure why, because it's not like there are sharks in any of our lakes. It makes almost as little sense as our middle-school team, the Lakeville Pirates. I feel like whoever came up with our team names doesn't get how lakes work.

Anyway, at our football games, someone gets to dress up in a shark costume and dance around on the sidelines; the guy who did it last year graduated, so the job is open. I've decided to try out, because it seems like a great way to impress people. For one thing, everyone pretty much has to cheer for you, so that'll automatically make them like you more. And for another, you get to spend the whole game hanging out with the cheerleaders on the sidelines. What could be wrong with that?

I've been doing research into mascots to get ready for my audition. I think the mascot that weirds me out the most is Mr. Met.

It seems to me that if you have a baseball for a head, the last place you're going to want to hang out is a ballpark full of men holding bats.

I bet a lot more people would be into model trains if they called them "mouse trains."

I don't think my English teacher, Mrs. Reddy, likes me. She told me today that I have "trouble seeing the forest for the trees." And I said, "I don't know what you mean. Aren't forests made up of trees?" And she said, "Yes, but sometimes, if you focus too much on one tree, you won't see the whole forest." And I said, "But if you're looking at a tree, then you're still technically looking at a forest. And probably your peripheral vision is picking up a lot more trees and undergrowth and other stuff." And I started to draw her a diagram of what I meant, and she said, "This is exactly what I'm talking about."

SEPTEMBER 24 [mood:  sharky]

I spent a lot of time in my room this afternoon getting ready for Wednesday's audition. I was jumping around and growling, and my little sister Sophie asked what I was doing, and I told her, "I'm getting ready to try out to be a shark." And she said, "Sharks don't growl." And I said, "Well, what noise do they make?" And she said, "They don't. They live underwater."

I hate when Sophie is right about stuff. But I'm gonna growl anyway.

[mood: excited] SEPTEMBER 25

Well, I went in for the mascot audition today, and it turns out, the competition wasn't that stiff. Only five guys showed up, and two of them were too tall for the costume, one of them was too short for it, and one of them couldn't do any games that fell on Saturdays because he has violin lessons then. And so they just gave me the job. I said, "Don't you want to see my shark moves?" And the head cheerleader, Alexandra McNeill, said, "Oh, we'll teach you all the routines you need to know."

Routines?

Uggggggggh. I just spent three hours after school with Alexandra and her cheerleading cocaptains as they tried to teach me all the steps for the shark-dance routines. I don't know how I never noticed this, but the shark doesn't just get to jump around and wave—there are, like, really elaborate dance moves involved in being the mascot. And while you'd think it'd be kind of fun to hang out with three cheerleaders, it's not actually all that enjoyable when all they're doing is shouting at

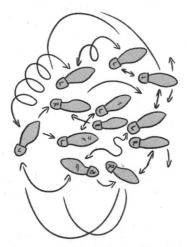

What I'm Supposed to Do

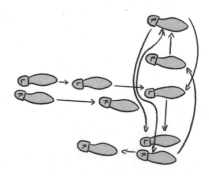

What I've Been Doing

you because you aren't dancing right. I think they think I'm stupid. At one point, I heard Alexandra whisper to the others, "I can't believe he's this A-W-F-U-L." And I said, "I can understand when you spell words out."

SEPTEMBER 28 [mood: mixed]

So today was the big football game, and I realized pretty quickly that the shark costume has four big downsides:

1. It's heavy and hard to see out of, which made it difficult to do the dance moves. The cheerleaders kept getting angry with me for being "two steps behind," even though I pointed out that maybe the problem was that they were two steps ahead.

2. The costume gets super hot on the inside, which makes you sweat a lot, which wouldn't be so bad, except that . . .

3. . . . the costume isn't washed all that

often, so it smells like other people's sweat. It was like spending a day inside a giant gym sock. I heard one person say after I walked past, "An actual dead shark would smell better."

4. It's a shark costume, so little kids are terrified of it. They kept bursting into tears when I came near, and even when I tried to open the jaws so they could see that I was a person inside the suit, that just made them cry more. I think they may've thought that I was someone the shark had eaten who was stuck in his throat.

By the end of the game, I was pretty miserable. But then, as we went into the locker room, I ran into the East Lakeville Dolphin. (They *really* don't understand how lakes work around here.) And a girl's voice from inside it said, "Hi! I hope those cheerleaders weren't too mean to you." And we talked for a little bit, and she seemed really nice. Her name's Megan, and she offered to meet up and give me some mascot pointers. So we made plans for next Saturday at the mall food court.

Oh, crap. I just realized I have no idea what she looks like. Unless she shows up dressed like this:

October

Here's something I've never understood about bakeries: Why don't they ever just leave loaves of bread in the oven for a few extra minutes, so that they become loaves of toast?

I'd much rather eat a loaf of toast.

So this morning, I told my parents they need to drive me to the mall on Saturday to hang out with Megan. And my mom said, "Oh, wow! My son's going on his first date!" And I said, "It's not a date!" And my dad said, "It's you and a girl meeting up and hanging out. That sure sounds like a date to me." And my mom said, "Let me ask you: Did she use the word *date* anywhere when she asked you to go?" And I thought about our conversation, and said, "Well, she *did* say, 'It's a date.' Does that mean anything?" And then my mom and dad both cracked up, and I realized: it's a date. I'm going on a full-fledged, official date. Apparently.

Now I'm super nervous.

Ugh. Ever since my parents told me that I'm going on a date on Saturday, I've been really anxious about it. I thought it'd just be hanging out, like when I went ice-skating with Jenny Bachman—the word *date* just makes it seem so formal. I'm trying to figure out if there's a way to make it less formal—I thought about bringing Chuck along, but my parents said bringing a friend to a date is a bad idea.

OCTOBER 4 [mood: distracted]

This whole date thing has me totally distracted. I keep wondering about stuff like, Do I have to pay for everything? What if she's already bought some food when I get there? Do I have to reimburse her? And what if she wants to split, like, a Cinnabon or something? I hate sharing food, because you always get to a point where each of you has eaten, like, two-fifths of something, and then there's one-fifth left on the plate and neither of you wants to finish it. It's terrible.

I've spent so much time thinking about stuff like that, I haven't been paying attention in school. I flunked a pop quiz about the Supreme Court in history class today, because I hadn't done any of the reading. Although I think I deserved partial credit for some of my answers:

Question 7: What is Justice Warren Burger known for?

He is Mayor McCheese's more successful brother.

OCTOBER 5 [mood: ow]

2:37 p.m.

I'm so nervous about this date, it makes my stomach hurt. When I told my parents that, my mom said, "It's just butterflies in your stomach." Which is an image that only makes my stomach hurt worse.

5:45 p.m.

Well, I'm off to my date. I'm sweating just thinking about it. My mom says that I have nothing to worry about—I just need to be myself. And also be polite, stand up straight, don't talk too much about myself, hold the door open, make eye contact, and not fidget or itch too much. Which is pretty much the opposite of what I consider "being myself." No wonder my stomach still hurts.

[mood: tired] **OCTOBER 10**

Sorry I haven't written in a few days. My date was a whole lot shorter than planned. I met up with Megan in the food court, and then, when we were in line for a pretzel, I threw up and passed out. It turns out that pain in my stomach was appendicitis, and I had to be rushed to the hospital to have my appendix removed. My dad said, "Why didn't you tell us you didn't feel well?" And I said, "I did! A bunch of times!" And then he said, "Oh, yeah . . . right. I guess you did. Sorry."

OCTOBER 11 [mood: better]

Megan came to visit me in the hospital today. She'd stopped at the cafeteria and picked us up two cups of Jell-O. "I hope you don't mind that I got two," she said. "I find sharing stuff kind of weird." And then we watched a DVD about famous mascots that she'd brought. It was actually kind of nice.

I've got one more day left in the hospital, and then I get to go home. It's been kind of boring here. Today I watched a marathon of the Superman movies on TV. Here's what I can't figure out about Superman: He has super hearing, so he can hear when people are in trouble, right? So anytime we see Clark Kent hanging out in the offices of the *Daily Planet*, or going on a date with Lois Lane, is it safe to assume that somewhere in Metropolis, there's someone getting beaten up or robbed and wondering what they ever did to tick off Superman?

On the bright side, I talked on the phone a little with Megan today. We made plans to meet up on Sunday and go see a movie—I suggested *Zombie Slayer III: The Reckoning,* and she seemed really excited about it, so I guess that's what we'll be seeing.

OCTOBER 14 [mood: happy]

So Megan and I went to the movies today. It turns out that I misunderstood her the other day: when I suggested *Zombie Slayer III*, she said, "That looks totally gruesome," and I thought that meant she was interested, but it turns out that, for her, "gruesome" is not a good thing. So instead we went and saw some dumb romantic comedy about a woman who plans weddings, who winds up falling in love with a guy who plans funerals.

Afterward, she asked how I liked it, and I said it was sort of predictable. And she said, "What do you mean?" And I said, "Well, you know the two people on the poster are going to wind up falling in love." And she said, "Well, yeah, I guess. But it's no more predictable than *Zombie Slayer.* I mean, you know he's going to slay all the zombies." And I suppose she's right. I guess the difference is, I'm much more interested in seeing someone kill zombies than in seeing two people fall in love.

After that, we walked around the mall awhile, and ate free food samples at Williams-Sonoma until the store manager asked us to leave. It was nice, I guess, but we didn't really have much to talk about. Like, we'd already told each other about our families and stuff, and I tried talking to her about video games, but she doesn't play any, and she tried to talk to me about the bands she likes, but I hadn't heard of any of them. And she didn't seem to get many of my jokes—like, when I pointed to the Banana Republic and said, "I don't know why they called the store that. I bet they get a lot of confused monkeys in there." And she said, "Monkeys can't read."

I was actually kind of relieved when it was time

for our parents to pick us up, but then, just as we were heading for the mall entrance, she started talking about what we could do the next time we hung out. And I realized that I had to tell her that I didn't want to go on another date with her. So I said, "Megan, I like you, but—" And she said, "I like you, too." And I was so startled I didn't say anything, and then she leaned in and kissed me! Right in front of the Lady Foot Locker! And then she said, "Let's do this again next weekend, OK?"

I'm not sure how it happened, but I think I have a girlfriend now?

OCTOBER 15 [mood: anxious]

So tonight I got a ton of texts from Megan—like, one after the other, telling me everything she was doing, as she was doing it. I told her that I shouldn't be using my phone for texting, so then she called me, and we wound up talking for an hour. I kept trying to say good-bye, but she kept on telling me all about her day and her friends and stuff. After a while, I just said *uh-huh* every minute or two to let her know that I was still there. It worked, mostly, except for when she asked why I had said *uh-huh* when she'd asked if I could think of anyone I'd rather spend time with than her.

I don't know what to do about Megan. She seems nice, and I don't want to be mean, but at the same time, I feel like, sooner or later, I'm going to have to tell her I don't want to go out with her. Because what's the other possibility? That we just keep dating, and eventually get married, and then, decades later, we die and get buried side by side?

That doesn't seem like a good plan.

7:47 p.m.

Talked to my dad tonight about Megan. He said if I don't want to go out with her, I need to just be direct and tell her. I asked him if he'd ever broken up with someone, and he said, "Yeah, back in high school, a bunch of times." Which is when my mom came in and said, "A bunch of times? Really? How come I've never heard about this?" And my dad suddenly got really interested in helping Sophie with her homework. Then my mom told me that if I'm going to break up with Megan, I should do it in person, or at least over the phone. "You can't break up with someone in a text," she said. "Just be nice about it, and tell her that it's not her, it's you."

So I guess I'm going to call Megan now and tell her that I'm not—

Hang on. I just got a text from Megan.

8:06 p.m.

Um . . . so, Megan just texted to say that she's really sorry, but she can't go out with me anymore. I guess she broke up with the guy who's the West

Lakeville Sea Turtle a few weeks ago, but now he wants to get back together with her. I wrote back, "That's fine." And she wrote, "It's nothing personal." And I wrote, "Really, it's fine." And she wrote, "It's just that I think I have more in common with him." And I wrote back, "You can stop now." And she wrote, "It's just, I thought you were a little boring." And I wrote back, "OK, I need to go do homework now."

I told my parents. I said that I'm sort of hurt, but mostly relieved. And my mom said, "I can't believe she broke up with you in a text." And my dad said, "Yeah. But look at it this way—you could've had a broken heart. All she cost you was a ruptured appendix."

I hadn't thought of it that way, but he was right.

OCTOBER 17   [mood: dread]

Ugh. This afternoon, these signs went up all around school:

And some of the older kids told me

The magic is in YOU

FUN ASSEMBLY!!
NEXT THURSDAY!!
ATTENDANCE IS
MANDATORY!!!

what it meant: One of the school guidance coun-
selors, Mr. Burke, is really into magic. And every
year, he leads a school-wide assembly in which he
does his stupid magic tricks, while talking about
the importance of self-esteem.

Everyone hates it, but no one's ever tried to
stop it. I guess when you're the amateur-magician
guidance counselor of a high school, your power
knows no bounds.

OCTOBER 18   [mood: thoughtful]

I was looking at the magic poster today
and realized what a weird term *top hat* is.
Pretty much all hats are top hats, because
they go on top of your head. If something
were a bottom hat, it'd be called a shoe.

[mood: tired]   OCTOBER 21

Today on the bus ride home, Chuck, Kevin, and
I were talking about Mr. Burke's stupid magic

assembly. And Chuck said, "I wish I could skip it." And Kevin said, "Yeah, but we'll get detention." And I said, "You know what'd be funny? If everyone in the school skipped it. I mean, they can't give all of us detention, right?" And then I went back to playing on my GamePort, but when I looked up, Chuck and Kevin were staring at me. And Chuck said, "That's brilliant!" And Kevin said, "You're a genius!" I'm not sure what they were talking about, but I had to get out because it was my stop. Still, it's always nice to be called a genius.

OCTOBER 22 [mood: alarmed]

So the first thing that happened when I showed up at school today was that Beverly Hsu—who's never spoken to me before—came over and said, "Tad! I'm in!" And I said, "Good! What are you talking about?" And she said, "Your plan for everyone to skip the assembly. I'm on board, and so is everyone else on the yearbook staff!" And I said, "How'd you find out about that?" And she said, "Everybody knows about it."

I guess after we all went home last night, Kevin texted my idea to his teammates on the school's soccer team, and then they all texted it to their friends, and by this morning, it had gotten around the whole school. I could hardly get to homeroom, because people kept stopping me and whispering that they thought skipping the assembly was a great idea, and they wished they'd thought of it themselves.

It was really nice, except for the fact that I was scared I'd get in trouble for it. All morning long, I kept waiting to get paged to the principal's office, but it never happened. And then at lunch, Mr. Burke came over to my table and said, "So, are you boys excited about the assembly?" and I froze in panic and couldn't say anything. Luckily, I didn't have to, because as soon as he asked the question, Chuck was trying so hard not to laugh that he inhaled a tater tot and it came out his nose.

OCTOBER 23   [mood: panicked]

So tomorrow's the big magic assembly, and as best I can tell, everyone's going to skip it. I'm also now 100 percent positive that I'm going to get in trouble for it. In English, Mrs. Reddy said, "I heard there might be some sort of plan afoot for tomorrow's assembly. Does anyone here know anything about it?" And I could swear she was looking right at me when she said it.

Meanwhile, everyone in my class is treating me like a hero for coming up with the plan. Bryce Dawson, our football team's quarterback, came by my locker to tell me, "I had no idea you were such a rebel." And Emily Sawicki told me I was a true revolutionary, like Che Guevara. I'm not sure who that is, but I think she meant it as a compliment. But if Bryce and Emily know it was my idea, then it's only a matter of time till Mr. Burke finds out.

OCTOBER 24 [mood: weird]

Well, today was a little crazy. I spent last night freaking out about how much trouble I'd get into if I was found out as the leader of the assembly skipping. And then, around one a.m., I realized something: if I actually attend the assembly, I'll be fine. After all, they can't punish me for what everyone else did, right?

So after lunch, when it was time for the assembly, I sneaked away from everyone who was sneaking away from the assembly, went to the gym, and took my seat.

And I was the only person there.

Well, not completely. Mr. Burke was there, with all his magic equipment. And after a minute or two, Doug Spivak came in. He sat down next to me and said, "Is this the assembly about magical skipping that everyone was talking about?"

But we were the only two people there. Once Mr. Burke realized what was going on, he sent some teachers to track down where everyone was hiding, and he said to us, "Well, since you two decided to actually attend the show, I've got a treat: you can be my assistants!"

And so—as one group of kids after another got rounded up by teachers and marched into the assembly—Doug and I had to stand onstage and help him with his stupid tricks. The worst part about it wasn't even the fact that I had to be onstage, picking cards out of the deck or helping to saw Doug in half as he lay down in a giant box labeled "PEER PRESSURE." It was the fact that, from the stage, I could watch everyone's faces as they came in and saw me up there. Some of them looked surprised. Some looked disappointed. Some of them looked angry. But none of them—not a single one—looked happy.

For Halloween, my dad and I helped Sophie make a jack-o'-lantern tonight. We'd already carved the mouth, nose, and one of the eyes when Sophie shouted, "Stop! It's perfect! Just get some red food coloring!" So this is what our jack-o'-lantern looks like:

Sophie's kind of a sick genius.

One day till Halloween. Went with my mom to the store to buy candy. She wanted to get candy corn, but I talked her out of it, because candy corn is the grossest candy. It tastes like slimy sugar, and it doesn't even look like corn. If anything, it looks like a bag of tiny traffic cones, or horribly diseased teeth.

OCTOBER 31 [mood: tricked, treated]

So my parents made me take Sophie trick-or-treating tonight. She was really smart about it, because she dressed as a vampire. Which, it turns out, is a costume you can pretty easily turn into a witch costume just by taking out the fangs, and adding a hat and a fake nose:

So each time we finished a block, Sophie would change costumes, go back to the start, and hit the houses with good candy a second time. I asked her if our mom and dad knew she was doing this, and she gave me a few full-sized Snickers bars and said, "Let's just keep it our little secret."

November

Who was on pennies before Lincoln was president? Were they just blank? Or was there some guy who was really happy to be on the penny, and then people had to come to him and go, "Hey, sorry, but . . . we're gonna replace you, 'cause, you know . . . now there's Lincoln"?

So today in geometry class, Mr. Schwartz was out sick, and we had a substitute teacher, Ms. Graham. When she started taking attendance, Chuck and I did what we always do when we get a sub, and traded names. We do this for two reasons:

1. It always cracks us up when substitute teachers call us by the wrong names, and:

2. We figure it's good practice in case we ever wind up becoming spies, because it's actually kind of tricky to remember not to answer when your own name is called, and to answer to someone else's name instead.

UNITED STATES OF AMERICA

"CHUCK SMITH"
27 OCT 1982
CALIFORNIA USA
NOV 17, 2013
NOV 16, 2018

USA

P<CHUCK <SMITH <<<<<<<<<<<<<<<<<<<

As it turned out, Ms. Graham wound up calling me "Chuck" a lot today, because she didn't know how to work the overhead projector, and so I had to help her with it. In fact, I felt kind of bad by the end of class, because as I was leaving, she said, "You know, it's hard being a substitute teacher, but everyone at this school seems really nice. Thanks for all your help, Chuck."

NOVEMBER 5 [mood: annoyed]

Bad news. Chuck was out sick today. Which wouldn't be a problem, except that Mr. Schwartz is also out sick, which means that Ms. Graham was subbing again today. And when she was taking attendance, she said, "I remember you, Chuck," and marked Chuck as being present. And that's when I realized: if I don't say anything when she calls my name, then she'll mark me as being absent, and I'll get a detention for skipping class. But if I confess that we switched names, then both Chuck and I will get detentions for messing with a sub. So in order to keep Chuck out of detention, I kept pretending to be him today. But he owes me one. I called him to tell him that, but his mom said that he couldn't come to the phone, because he was puking.

[mood: frustrated] **NOVEMBER 6**

Arrrrrgh. Chuck was out sick *again* today, and Mr. Schwartz still isn't back, so Ms. Graham marked me absent from math a second time, even though I was sitting right there. I've now got *two* days of detention, and it's getting really hard to remember to answer whenever she calls Chuck's name.

I'm thinking that as funny as it was to hear her to call Chuck "Tad" and me "Chuck" a few times on Monday, and as nice as it was to get some spy practice in, it really wasn't worth it.

NOVEMBER 7 [mood: embarrassed]

Well, today, I couldn't take it anymore. Chuck was out sick again today, and Ms. Graham was still subbing in math. And I realized: at this rate, I'm up to three days of detention—and counting—for skipping class, versus Chuck and I doing one day of detention together for swapping names. So I went up to Ms. Graham after class and told her: "My name's not Chuck. It's Tad. I'm really sorry, but my friend and I switched names on your first day." And she said, "Yeah, I know. I knew it all along. I've been marking you 'present'—I was just waiting to see how long it'd take before you confessed." I asked her how she knew, and she said, "Um, you've

got your name written on your backpack. And your notebook. And your calculator. Also, your friends have all been calling you Tad, and you put your own name on the homework you handed in yesterday."

I'm beginning to realize that maybe I wouldn't be a very good spy.

NOVEMBER 8   [mood: annoyed]

I feel like, if the only kind of pencil anyone ever uses is the No. 2 pencil, then that pencil should be called the No. 1 pencil.

So I've gotten to like Ms. Graham a lot—she's nice, and funny, and she didn't get me in trouble for switching names with Chuck. And today, she told us that she had good news: Mr. Schwartz will be out for the rest of the year, so she'll keep teaching us. Everyone was really happy about it. Even Mr. Perkins, our biology teacher, was happy about it—I saw him come up to Ms. Graham and tell her how happy he was that she's staying. Which seemed sort of weird—why would he care? She's not even a science teacher.

NOVEMBER 12 [mood: surprised]

So tonight, my parents took Sophie and me to the mall, to get dinner at the Outback Steakhouse. It was fun, even though I don't think there's a single more disgusting name for a food than "baby back ribs."

BABY → BACK → RIBS →

But the oddest part was that as we were leaving, I saw Ms. Graham coming into the restaurant with Mr. Perkins. I tried to say hi to them, but I guess they didn't see me, even though I could've sworn Mr. Perkins was looking right at me when I was waving hello. It was weird.

[mood: sleepy] **NOVEMBER 13**

So today in math class, I told Ms. Graham that I saw her at the Outback Steakhouse with Mr. Perkins. She said, "Oh! You did? That's nice. He and I were talking about, um, school stuff." And I told her that that's what I figured, but I was surprised the school nurse, Miss Tibbetts, wasn't there. And she said, "Why would Miss Tibbetts be there?" And I said, "Oh, she and Mr. Perkins are good friends. He sometimes gives her a ride to school in the morning." And she said, "Really." But not like it was a question, like it was a sentence. Anyway, I said that now that she knows Mr. Perkins and Miss Tibbetts are friends, the three of them can all hang out. And she said, "Yes. That'd be interesting."

the yard. I hate raking leaves more than just about anything. For one thing, the rakes are always somehow behind everything else in the garage, so before I could even start, I had to pull all the other junk out of the garage, and then untangle the rakes from a bunch of extension cords.

Then, I spent an hour and a half raking up all the leaves, putting them into piles, and bagging them. And just when I came back inside and sat down to play video games, my dad came home and shouted, "Tad! I told you to rake the leaves!" And I looked outside and saw: a big wind had come along and blown a lot more leaves off the trees, and blown some of the neighbors' leaves onto our lawn, too. It was like the world had hit CTRL-Z on an hour and a half of work.

I swear, one day, I'm going to sell a product called "tree nets." They're like hairnets for trees—you just

Anyway, when I walked past Mr. Perkins's room later, I saw the two of them having a really intense conversation. I heard Ms. Graham say Miss Tibbetts's name, so I bet that they were making plans to hang out soon.

NOVEMBER 14 [mood: disgusted]

Rough biology class today. We were dissecting earthworms, and Mr. Perkins decided that he'd assign one kid at random to clean out all the worm-dissection trays, and somehow, I was the one he picked. The strange thing was, he didn't draw names out of a hat or anything. He just said, "I'm picking one person at random. Tad."

Anyway. I think I've still got worm guts under my fingernails.

NOVEMBER 17 [mood: anno

Well, I'd been putting it off and putting it off, bu today my dad made me rake up all the leaves i

put them on in September, and pull them off in December.

And then, with all the money I make from selling tree nets, I'm going to move to a house surrounded by nothing but cacti.

I wonder why the pilgrims had buckles on their hats.

Was it so that they could adjust them, in case their heads shrank?

It's weird how many toy commercials end with "batteries sold separately," but battery commercials never end with "toy sold separately."

Our school had a field trip to see an orchestra perform tonight. I can never really pay attention to classical music—my mind always winds up wandering. Tonight, I spent most of my time wondering whether the guy who plays the triangle gets paid less than the rest of the orchestra. I mean, he has to stand there for the same amount of time as everyone else, but I bet the violin players must hate him.

8:15 p.m.

Ugh. Tonight, my mom went to get the Thanksgiving turkey out of the freezer in the garage, where she'd been keeping it. And I guess when I was getting the rake out of the garage the other day, and untangling all the cords, I must've pulled out the plug to the freezer, because the turkey's completely thawed out, and it's gone bad. I asked my mom if she was sure, and she said, "Come smell this." And yeah. It had gone bad.

We went to four stores looking for a turkey, but they're all out. We may not have a Thanksgiving dinner tomorrow. I keep wanting to point out that none of this would've happened if my dad hadn't made me rake the leaves, but it doesn't seem like the time for it.

8:47 p.m.

Good news! My mom was just talking to her friend Brenda, from her book club, and mentioned what had happened to the turkey. And she said that Brenda invited us to have Thanksgiving with her family! Sophie said, "Is Brenda the one with the sparkly cat sweaters?" And my dad said, "No, Brenda's the one who wears way too much perfume." And I said, "No, I think she's the one who hugs hello and holds the hug too long and makes you uncomfortable." And my mom said, "Actually, she's not any of those. Brenda's the one who knits all her own clothing. And it was very nice of her to invite us." And my dad said, "Brenda's . . . a little odd." And my mom said, "I know. Just . . . it'll be fine. I'm sure she has a lovely husband, and we'll have a nice time. It'll be fine. It'll be fine." Somehow, each time my mom said, "It'll be fine," I got half as sure that it'll be fine.

NOVEMBER 28 [mood: gobble, gobble]

So guess what? Between the two of them, Brenda and her husband are deathly allergic to gluten, soy, potatoes, carrots, and nuts. Also, they're vegans. So Thanksgiving consisted of a football-shaped thing that they sliced and gave us. I asked what it was, and Brenda said, "It's Satan!" But it turns out what she meant was, it's seitan. Which I guess is some sort of fake meat thing? They also had a pureed cauliflower and green-bean thing that looked, as Sophie said, "like

someone put a frog in a blender." I ate a few bites of each, but couldn't keep going. And then my mom whispered under her breath, "Tad, you need to eat at least a few bites of it." And Brenda said, "What was that?" And I said, "My mom was saying this is so delicious, she wants seconds!" And Brenda said, "Oh, that's wonderful!" And I said, "Here, Mom— let me help you," grabbed the serving platter with one hand, and then pushed some of my seitan loaf onto her plate with the other.

After dinner, Brenda's husband started talking

about diseases of the lower intestine. He seemed really knowledgeable about it, and my dad said, "Are you a doctor?" And he said, "No, just an enthusiast." And then he went to get some medical diagrams to show us, and my dad said, "Well, we should get going. It's the kids' bedtime." And I said, "It's 8:00 p.m.—" and was about to say, "This hasn't been my bedtime in years," when my dad shot me a look. And so I just started yawning, and my mom said, "Oh, yes, we should get them home."

On the way back, we stopped at a convenience store and bought some sliced turkey and a loaf of bread. When we got home, my dad peeled some potatoes, boiled and mashed them, and my mom made some stuffing from a box, while Sophie and I put together turkey sandwiches.

And that's when we learned the true meaning of Thanksgiving, because I'd never been more thankful for a meal in my whole life.

December

Today Mr. Wilson, the history teacher, told us we could sign up for Model UN. Chuck and I got all excited until Mr. Wilson explained that it wasn't actually a United Nations made up of models. Too bad. I think that's a really good idea.

So Christmas is just a little more than three weeks away, and I know what I want: An X-Blast 3-D Video Console Gaming System. I've been trying to drop little hints about it—like, I've been leaving newspapers and magazines open to ads for it. And anytime we're watching TV, and my dad is fast-forwarding through commercials, I'll make him stop and watch the X-Blast Gaming System ads, and then I'll say, "Cool! I bet one of those would be a lot of fun to have!"

You know—subtle stuff like that.

[mood: psyched] DECEMBER 4

So today at lunch, Mr. Hoover, my gym teacher, announced that he would be handling the sign-up sheet for the ninth-grade talent show next week. And I didn't tell any of my friends, but I went up to him afterward and signed up. I've been working on some pretty good celebrity impressions, and I want to surprise people with them.

If I had to play an instrument, I think I would play the bagpipes, because if I did it badly, no one would be able to tell.

At lunch today, Chuck and Kevin were talking about the talent show, and saying how they were wondering what people would do. They were pretty sure that Courtney Clark would do some kind of gymnastics routine, and Amanda Haller would try and sing, and maybe Brian Timmins would juggle. But none of them even guessed that I might be doing something! It's gonna be awesome when they see what I've got planned.

DECEMBER 8 [mood: concerned]

So tonight, after dinner, I decided to tell my parents about my celebrity impressions for the talent show. And my mom said, "I didn't even know you could do celebrity impressions!" And my dad said, "Let's hear one!" And so I said, in my Shia LaBeouf voice, "Guess who this is?" And my mom said, "Um, I don't know." And my dad said, "Was that an impression?" And I said, "It was Shia LaBeouf! I sounded just like him!" And my mom said, "You know, he doesn't really have that distinctive a voice. . . ." And so then I did it again, but this time, I said, "I'm Shia LaBeouf, the star of the *Transformers* movies." And my mom said, "Ohhhh . . . yeah, I guess I can hear that now."

And my dad said, "Maybe you should try someone with a more distinctive voice, like Bugs Bunny, or Darth Vader, or something." And I said, "Everyone can do those! I'm doing the really hard ones." So I tried a bunch more impressions on them—Leonardo DiCaprio, Ryan Reynolds, Ben Affleck—but it seemed like they only really could figure out who I was trying to impersonate if I started my impression by saying, "I'm—" and then filling in the name of the person.

Still, I'm guessing that's just my parents and their old ears. I think my impressions are great, and I bet everyone at school will, too.

DECEMBER 10 [mood: ambivalent]

Today was the talent show. It got off to kind of a slow start. As we'd expected, Courtney Clark did one of her gymnastics routines. And Alana James played her violin, and Todd Nguyen and Jeff Blanchard did a funny ventriloquist routine where Jeff sat on Todd's lap and

pretended to be a dummy. And then Doug Spivak came out to show off his talent: "I can call whether a coin is going to be heads or tails while it's still in the air and be right, like, almost half the time." And then he threw a quarter in the air, but he lost sight of it, and spent about five minutes crawling around on the stage on his hands and knees looking for it before Mr. Hoover told him we had to move on.

And then it was my turn. And I came out, and I started with my best impression: Ryan Reynolds, from the *Green Lantern* movie. And the room was super quiet. And at first I thought the microphone didn't work, but when I asked if it was working, everyone shouted, "Yes!" And so I tried a few more of my impressions—Sam Worthington, Jon Cryer, Ryan Seacrest—and still, nothing. And I suddenly realized that I was doing even worse than Doug Spivak, and I started to sweat horribly.

And then I looked around the room and saw

the teachers standing in the back, and I realized: there were some people I could impersonate who everyone would know immediately. So I said, in my best Mr. Burke voice, "Hey, kids! Who's interested in the magic that's inside you?" And everyone started laughing. And then I started imitating all the school's teachers—Miss Pethoukis's odd, raspy voice, Mr. Webster's weird habit of making every sentence sound like a question, Miss Delacroix's French accent—everything I could think of. And by the end of it, when Mr. Hoover asked people to applaud for their favorite act, everyone cheered the loudest for me.

Except for the teachers. They looked kind of angry. And afterward, Mr. Hoover came over and said, "Congratulations. You just won the talent show, and detention tomorrow."

And you know what?

It was totally worth it.

DECEMBER 11   [mood: grossed out]

Today I served my detention. It was kind of weird— I've never gotten detention before. I was assigned to "lunch detention," which means you have to get your lunch, then go eat quietly in Mr. Perkins's room for the whole lunch period. You're not allowed to read anything fun, or nap, or draw anything. You're allowed to do your homework, and eat lunch, and that's it.

None of which would be that bad, except that the room's totally quiet, and Mr. Perkins has this weird thing where he clears his throat and makes a really gross phlegmy noise—like a super loud *snrk!*—every thirteen seconds. I know it's every thirteen seconds because, once I started noticing it, I couldn't  pay attention to anything else. It was impossible to read or do homework, and definitely made it impossible to eat, because it was such a disgusting noise.

I talked about it afterward with the other kids in detention, and none of us could figure out: Does Mr. Perkins not know that he makes that noise?

Or does he know it, and that's why he volunteered for detention—because he knows it's so unbearable that you'll do anything never to get put in a silent room with him again?

Anyway, one of the other people in detention was Dean Bartlett, who's the goalie on our school's hockey team. He's a freshman, even though he's sixteen, because he got held back a few times. And he's huge, and kind of mean. And he came up to me after detention and said, "I saw you were doing your geometry homework in there. Are you good at it?" And I said, "I'm pretty good." And he said, "Awesome. Coach says I need to get my average above a C in order to keep playing. So you're gonna be my study buddy." And I said, "You mean, like, helping you with homework and stuff?" And he said, "No, I mean doing my homework. And sitting close enough to me during tests that I can copy off of you." And I said, "What if I don't want to do that?" And he said, "Then I'll break your collarbone. Why? Do you not want to do that?" And I said, "No! I was just curious."

Anyway. I should go work on my geometry assignment for tomorrow. And then, I guess, work on it again with slightly different handwriting.

So I brought Dean his homework today. And he looked at it and said, "Hang on. Give me your assignment." And I did, and then he erased one of my answers and wrote in a wrong one. "There!" he said. "If our homework's identical, Ms. Graham might get suspicious." And I said, "Why did mine have to be the one with the wrong answer?" And he said, "Because you like having all your teeth." Which seemed like a pretty good answer, actually.

[mood: alarmed] DECEMBER 13

We got our geometry assignments back today. Dean got an A-minus, and—thanks to the answer he changed—I got a B-plus. Dean took me aside after class and said, "Look, an A-minus is nice, but I think, if you really apply yourself, you can get me an A." It's weird that he has such high standards for work he isn't doing.

DECEMBER 14   [mood: hopeful]

At dinner tonight, I spent awhile talking about the X-Blast Gaming System, telling my parents about how it's the most sophisticated gaming system known to man, and how it'll really help me improve my hand-eye coordination, so it's practically an educational tool. And I think it's working, because right after dinner, I heard them talking quietly upstairs for a long time, so I bet they're figuring out when to get the system for me.

[mood: nauseated]   DECEMBER 15

Today my mom and Sophie made a gingerbread house to decorate our mantel. The creepy thing about a gingerbread house is, the house is made out of the exact same materials as the people. So I guess, to a gingerbread person, it's basically a house made out of their own flesh.

MUM? DAD?

DECEMBER 18 [mood: annoyed]

I was sitting home tonight, watching TV, when the phone rang. And it was Dean, calling me to remind me that "we" have a geometry test tomorrow, so he wanted to make sure that I was studying. So I guess I should start reviewing geometry for tomorrow, even though I'm actually just feeling sort of tired and achy.

[mood: terrible] DECEMBER 19

Ugh. I woke up this morning with a horrible sore throat and a fever, so I stayed home from school and slept. It's two o'clock and I just woke up and— uh-oh.

The geometry test.
I wonder how Dean did.

Well, today I was back at school, and I managed to avoid Dean all through the day, right up until final period, when I saw him in geometry. Afterward, Dean cornered me near my locker and lifted me up by my shirt. He said I was in big trouble for not being there for him on the test, but that he'd consider forgiving me if I wrote his *Huckleberry Finn* paper for his English class. I told him I wasn't even in that class, and he said, "Well, I guess you'd better start reading, then, 'cause it's due our first day back from Christmas break."

So today's the first day of break—Chuck and Kevin and I have already made a bunch of plans to hang out. Tomorrow, we're thinking of going to the mall, where Chuck's older brother Sid is working as a Christmas elf in Santa's Workshop. Chuck says Sid has to be "in character" at all times and pretend to be an elf named Bingo, so we wanted to go and see how much we can bother him before he finally snaps.

I asked my dad if he would take me to the mall, and he said he couldn't, because he and my mom had something they needed to do. And since it's not like them to be all secretive, I said, "Where are you guys going?" And my mom said, "It's just . . . an errand we need to run." And my dad said, "Don't worry. It's nothing bad." And then they smiled at each other.

And that's when I knew: they were going to Best Buy to get me the X-Blast Gaming System. There's just no other possibility I can think of.

DECEMBER 23 [mood: startled]

Well, tonight after dinner, my parents sat me and Sophie down and said, "We have some big, exciting news for you. We were going to wait until Christmas, but we couldn't wait." And Sophie said, "Are you getting a divorce?" And my mom said,

"No!" and my dad said, "Why would you even ask that?" And Sophie just sort of shrugged and said, "Lots of my friends' parents are getting one." Then my mom asked her what she thinks a divorce is, and Sophie said, "I don't know, but a lot of times, when people's parents get them, they wind up getting puppies."

Then my dad said, "Well, no, we're not getting divorced. But you two are getting—" And I said, "You got us an X-Blast 3-D Video Console Gaming System!" And my dad said, "Um, you're getting a little brother. Or a little sister. Your mother is pregnant." And I said, "But aren't you too old to have a baby?" and Sophie said, "I don't want a baby! I want a puppy! Why can't you guys just get divorced?" and went off to her room and slammed the door. That's when my mom turned to my dad and said, "You know, none of this is going the way I'd imagined."

DECEMBER 24   [mood: worried]

So I was hanging out with Chuck today. I told Chuck that my mom's going to have a baby, and he was like, "Wow. So, are you going to have to give up your room? When my baby sister was born, I had to start sharing a room with my little brother."

We don't have a third bedroom for the baby. I hadn't even thought of that. So at dinner tonight, I asked my parents, "Where's the new baby going to sleep?" And my dad said, "Well, we were thinking that, if it's a boy, it'll be in your room, and if it's a girl, it'll be in Sophie's." I asked how soon we can find out what the baby's going to be, and my mom said, "Don't you think it'll be fun to be surprised?" I don't think my mom and I have the same idea of what constitutes fun.

DECEMBER 25 [mood: humbug]

So today was Christmas, and the good news is, I got a whole bunch of games for the X-Blast 3-D Video Console Gaming System. And with each one I unwrapped, I got a little more excited, because I figured that my parents had actually gotten me the gaming system. But once I'd unwrapped everything, there was still no gaming system. And I said to my parents, "Um, where is it?" And my mom said, "Where is what?" And I said, "The gaming system. The one to play these games on." And my dad said, "Oof. Um . . . we thought you already had the system for these." And I said, "Why would you think that? We have the X-Tastic 3000HD Video Gaming Console System. That's a totally different thing! Weren't you paying attention when I was talking about it all this month?" And my dad said, "Well . . . we were a little distracted, what with the baby and all. . . ."

So I got to spend Christmas morning staring at games that I have no way of being able to play. I can't believe that my new sibling is messing up my life when he or she isn't even here yet.

DECEMBER 27   [mood: fuzzy]

My mom had an ultrasound today, and brought home a picture of the baby:

According to my mom, the blob at the right is the baby's head, and the stuff at the left is its legs. Or vice versa. I can't remember.

My mom said, "Don't you think it's cute?" and I noticed my dad standing behind her nodding yes, so I said it was cute.

I bet a really good business would be one where you pretend to have an ultrasound machine, and then just hand everyone the same blurry photo and tell them it's a picture of their baby. I don't know why nobody's thought of that.

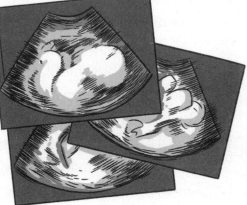

On second thought, maybe they have.

DECEMBER 28 [mood: upset]

Well, Sophie and I kept nagging my parents, and today, they agreed to call the doctor and find out if the baby is a girl or a boy.

And it's a boy.

Which means, I guess, I'll soon be sharing a room with a little brother.

So this morning at breakfast, we started talking about what to name my new brother. Sophie suggested naming him Justin Bieber. My dad said, "You mean Justin as his first name, and Bieber as his middle name?" And Sophie said, "No. Justin Bieber, period." I suggested naming him Lastname, because I think it'd be funny whenever someone asked for his first name if he said, "Lastname." My mom said, "Um, actually, we're leaning toward naming him after my father. So his name would be Fred." Which was a relief, because for a second there, I thought she meant they were going to name him Baby Grandpa.

So my dad talked to me today about the baby. He said, "How do you feel about being an older brother?" And I said, "I already *am* an older brother." And he said, "Oh. Right. But this won't be like Sophie. This'll be a little kid who needs someone to look up to, who can teach him right from wrong." And then he whispered, "Between you and me? I'm not sure I trust Sophie with that." And I said that yeah, I guessed I was ready for it.

And then my dad said, "Come down to the basement." And we walked into the rec room downstairs, where we keep our broken ping-pong table that we never use, and some old boxes of junk. And he said, "So, this is a pretty big room. And it gets some light from the windows near the ceiling. And your mom and I have been thinking— what would you say to having a little space of your own? We could clear out this room, and you'd have a whole private setup down here. Would you like that?"

And I said, "A private space that's two floors away from Sophie and a crying baby? What do you think?" And my dad smiled and said, "Yeah. I figured you'd say that."

DECEMBER 31 [mood: ready]

Well, I guess this marks the end of another year. I don't know what next year will bring, but I'm excited for it. I mean, for starters, I'll have a whole floor of the house to myself, which'll be fun. Plus, I'll have a little brother. And I've got a lot to teach him. I mean, just look at all the stuff I've learned this year. I learned how to ice-skate, and how to dance. I learned not to put a suit in the washing machine, and to always put eggs on top when bagging groceries. I learned where my appendix used to be, and where my high school's swimming pool isn't. And I learned to spell *prospicience*, even though I don't know what it means.

I did find myself thinking about what my dad said, though—about being a good role model for my little brother. And I've been thinking about what a lousy role model it'd make me if I kept letting

Dean Bartlett intimidate me into helping him cheat his way through high school. So tonight, I started work on his paper on *Huckleberry Finn*—I want to have it ready for him to hand in the day he gets back to school. Here's how it begins:

Huckleberry Finn *is the story of a huckleberry with a fin.*

I can't wait to see what grade Dean gets on it.